Elaine has writ
of her being. Sh
family, her friends, the way she speaks, the way she writes is all
done with passion. God has blessed her and has allowed her to
share one of her many talents with the world when she wrote
Nan's Journey.
Stacy Townsend

Elaine is one of the most thoughtful people I've ever known.
In addition, she's creative and outright fun! I'm not at all sur-
prised that she's also a successful author!
Chris Samples, President
Chris Samples Broadcasting, Inc.
98.3 KXDJ

Having pastored fifteen years, and as a lover of Christian fic-
tion for over thirty years, it has been a joy to read the very
moving story of Mrs. Littau's *Nan.* I look forward to her future
work and to the resolution of *Nan's Journey.*
R. Scott Barton
Senior Pastor of Harvest Time First Assembly of God
Church.

This intriguing story drew me in from the very beginning.
I "became" Nan trying to escape from a painful life. *Nan's
Journey* was full of excitement and hope for the future.
Geraldine Bond

Through Elaine's talent and imagination she has utilized her
creative nature in this book. Nan will capture your heart as
her life unfolds through sorrows and joys. Nan learns to love,
forgive, and trust God through unpredictable twists and turns.
This is a book I could not put down! I can't wait for the sequel.
Melissa Otto

NAN'S
JOURNEY

NAN'S
JOURNEY

by Elaine Littau

Joyce + Dave,
I love you guys.
Elaine Littau

Published by Tate Publishing & Enterprises, LLC
127 E. Trade Center Terrace | Mustang, Oklahoma 73064 USA
1.888.361.9473 | www.tatepublishing.com

Tate Publishing is committed to excellence in the publishing industry. The
company reflects the philosophy established by the founders, based on Psalms
68:11,
"The Lord gave the word and great was the company of those who published
it."

Published in the United States of America

ISBN: *978-1-60247-832-9*

1. Fiction/General/Romance
07.09.24

Dedication

This book is dedicated to my husband, Terry; sons, Stephen, Marlin, and Michael; daughters-in-law, Aimee and Cari; grandchildren, Devon, Zach, Sierra, and Maci; and siblings, Donna, Geraldine, Wanda, Maynard, and Jim.

Acknowledgements:

My mother and daddy had six children. I happen to be number six. When I came along my siblings were either teenagers or in their twenties. By the time I became a teenager my parents had retired.

My growing up years were flavored with many stories from my parents of "old times." They told of how both of them moved from Missouri, Kansas, Oklahoma, and Colorado in covered wagons. My grandparents were real pioneers, black-smiths, and homesteaders.

Westerns played on the television every evening as I did homework and books by Grace Livingston Hill, Zane Grey, and Louis L'Amour made up the majority of my entertainment selections. All of this was the basis of an appreciation of by-gone days. Today I can imagine myself bumping along on a wagon seat or gathering cow chips. Mother and Daddy are gone now, but the stories live on.

Foreword

There are people who flow in and out of our lives, weaving a beautiful tapestry of relationships, but sometimes you see the same colorful thread or pattern repeated over and over. That's how it is with a good friend. Their presence is woven into our lives until it literally becomes part of the pattern of our lives. Elaine Littau has been that kind of friend for me. She is a woman of many diverse, creative talents, not the least of which is the ability to take a negative situation and turn it into something positive and even wonderful. Elaine has a keen eye for possibility, an innate ability to take unlikely materials and mold them into beautiful creations. Throughout the years, I've known her to take on various challenges from set design for the community play, to Robin Hood costumes for the neighborhood boys to play in, to speaking before ladies' groups and creating crafts for the local craft cooperative, just to name a few. An artist, writer, humorist, and speaker, Elaine can fill many roles. She simply sees things differently than the rest of us. A crack in the wall? Well, we'll just paint over it thus and so, and voila! It looks like it was meant to be that way. Not enough money to purchase the right supplies? Let's try this and that, and suddenly, you have the intended effect. The word "impossible" is *not* in her vocabulary. A gifted story-teller, Elaine has a natural ability to make people laugh. Through the years, she has regaled her friends with stories of her wonderful husband and sons, and large extended family, complete with accents and colloquialisms. Many times, Elaine has taken an unpleasant incident and woven it into a hilarious tale, which ends more often than not with an imitation of her husband's slow Texas drawl, "Well, babe," as a preface to any explanation he feels the need to make. I recall her lively tale of working in the kitchen of a church camp one hot Georgia summer, and repeating a southern cook's drawled advice to her that "You cain't rosh aiggs," as she rushed about in the stifling humidity to crack and scramble enough eggs for a couple hundred hungry youngsters. Elaine's expressive mimicry and ability to paint pictures with words can make you see a scene so vividly in your mind that the experience seems to become your own. Elaine's giftings are God-designed and God-given, and those who know her have been blessed by those gifts, because she so generously shares herself with others. I hope that her story of *Nan's Journey* will inspire those who read it, and that Elaine's personal story will encourage others to take a chance and try what they've never tried before, and spread their wings and fly, even if just a little.

Rhonda Culwell

Chapter One

It was late. The moon had risen and the night symphony was in full force. Crickets chirped at their rivals, the frogs, and dominated the night chorus. Only one sound in the forest was foreign—a whimper from under the ferns. At the base of the largest pine in the woods was a small form crying, moaning, and whimpering. Black hair, matted and dirty, hung in long ropes down the front of the tiny girl. She had been in this spot for hours. At least that is what it felt like to her. Stretching, she cried out in pain. The blood-covered welts burst open to bleed again. Her back was wet with blood, and her dress was torn and useless.

Why had she dared to speak to the woman that she was obliged to call mother in that way? She knew that talking was not allowed from children before chores were finished. The accusations being made by "Ma" were totally false and she could not let Elmer take the blame for something she her-self had forgotten to do. She shut her eyes tight against the memory, but it intruded anyway.

She had just gotten up to take the water off the stove to make up dishwater for the supper dishes. Ma had stepped out-side the room to turn down her bed and prepare for sleep. When she reappeared in the kitchen, she realized that the wood supply next to the stove was low. Elmer was standing next to the table gathering the plates for washing. "Elmer, where is the wood you were supposed to bring up to the house?" Before he could answer, a hand had slapped him across his face. Getting back onto his feet and standing as tall as a five year old can stand, he looked her in the eye and said, "Ma, I was sick today, 'member?"

Elaine Littau

"So, Elmer, you're going to play up that headache trick again. Nan, didn't your good for nothing Mama teach you people how to work, or are you just lazy?"

"Our Mama was good! Don't you say mean things about her!" Nan yelled as her heart raced at the assault against her real Mama's character.

"What about it, Elmer, are you like your weakling Mama or what?" Elmer's eyes became very large and filled with tears. He could barely remember his real Mama, but when he did, he remembered soft kisses and sweet singing and a beautiful face. "I'm sorry; I'll get the wood now."

"No, Elmer, don't. I promised you I'd do it today when your head was hurting, but I forgot. I'll get it after I do these dishes."

"Listen here, Nan, I'm the boss around here and Elmer will do what I say, when I say, and you will respect me."

Nan's eyes widened.

"Don't look at me like that, little girl."

Nan held her breath.

"Well, I guess you will be making a trip to the wood shed...with me!" Ma had grabbed her by the arm and jerked her along behind the shed. The strap was hanging there, waiting. Whippings were becoming more and more frequent. After Ma's husband left, they had taken on a more cruel form. The last whipping was more like a beating. It took days for the marks to scab over and heal. Little Elmer had come in that night and brought some horse medicine from the barn and applied it to the oozing marks.

The next afternoon when the schoolteacher came over, Ma had already formulated a story. "Mrs. Dewey, we missed Nan and Elmer today at school. Are they sick?" Ma lied the first time in her life and said, "Well Miss Sergeant, since Mr. Dewey is going to be gone for another four weeks, I need more help around here to get things done. I'm holding the kids out until he gets back." Week after week went by, and Mr. Dewy still hadn't come home. Everyday Ma grew more and more angry. It became more and more impossible to please her. When she began hitting Elmer, it was too much. Nan had to do something—right or wrong; things couldn't stay the way they were.

The coolness of the earth had settled into Nan's bones. She stood silently for a minute and carefully crept up to the farmhouse. As she opened the door, she saw that Elmer was in the pallet at the foot of the stove next to her bedroll. Ma was asleep in her room. The door held open with a rock. Slowly she began peeling off the dress and the dried blood stuck to it. She reached for the old shirt she normally wore over her wounds and under her dress. She had washed it today. It had blood-stains on it, but it would keep her from ruining another dress. She retrieved the old work dress that she wore when chores were messier than usual; it was the only one left. She put it on swiftly and shook Elmer awake with her hand over his mouth. "Baby, we must leave. Do you understand? Stay quiet and I will get some stuff to take with us."

She found large old handkerchief and began looking for food supplies. There was one sourdough biscuit and about a cup of cold brown beans. She located her tin cup and another rag. She would probably need that. Three matches were in the cup on the stove. She would just take two. Suddenly she heard a sound from Ma's room. A scampering sound…just a rat. Ma turned over. Her breathing became deep and regular. For once Nan wished that Ma snored. She tied the handkerchief in a knot over the meager food supplies, grabbed their bedrolls, and slowly opened the door.

"Come on, Elmer. Can you carry this food? I'll get your bedding. That's a good boy. We must hurry!"

The cold air bit at their faces, but they walked bravely on.

"Elmer, we must go tonight so we can get as far away as we can before Ma wakes up and sees that we are gone."

For the next half hour the pair walked in silence through the familiar woods past the graves on the hill. In one, a mother dearly loved, in another, an infant who had died the same day as his mother, and the third, a father that only Nan had memory of. Elmer was only two years old when Pa died in the logging accident. Nan snapped out of her reverie and urged Elmer on. Molasses, Pa's good old workhorse, stood in the pasture. He skidded the logs Pa cut with his axe. His legs hadn't healed quite right, but Mama hadn't let Mr. Dewey kill him because he was all she had left of the husband of her youth. Molasses was a faithful friend to Nan and Elmer. He stood there and waited for them to mount him.

"Molasses, take us to…" Nan realized then that they had nowhere to go. Mrs. Dewey had said that they were ungrateful little imps who didn't realize she and Mr. Dewey were taking care of them out of kindness, and they could easily be put into an orphanage. Nan didn't know anything about orphanages except what Mrs. Dewey…uh, Ma had told her. "Molasses, just take us out of here."

Chapter Two

It felt good to be off her feet and sitting on the broad back of the faithful horse. Elmer was in front of her and she had him lean back against her so he could sleep. She wrapped them with the skimpy little bedrolls and rode into the night.

Once started, she allowed herself to think about the occupants of those graves and how her life had changed in the last five years. Thinking back, she remembered golden, happy days. The sky seemed so blue and the woods so fresh and pine scented. Pa was such a handsome man, tall, blonde and muscular. He wore the title of "man" with dignity, and strength. Mama had loved him so much. She called out to him and Nan as they were playing in the meadow. When she caught up to them, she showered them with kisses and hugs. Mama, a tiny woman with raven black hair, was strong and brave. Nan could remember her singing while she worked. She sang while she cooked, sewed, gardened, and even while she washed on the washboard. The melodies floated from her mouth on angel wings. Pa used to tell her that if he listened while he was in the woods, he would swear that the little birds were trying to send up a sweet offering to the Lord, but couldn't quite do it. Mama would say that her songs came from the blessing of God and a dear family. Mama had been an orphan. Nan had forgotten about that! Pa's mother and father had been dead a long time. As far and Nan knew, her only living relative was her little brother.

Nan remembered when the singing stopped. The day had been beautiful. Pa was logging. His helper had been helping him skid the logs. He had piled them high. Pa was trying to get them loaded on the wagon to go to the mill. The logs rolled on top of him. They crushed him, and he died three days later. Mama tried to keep food on the table. Everyone else in the woods was poor, too. When Mr. Dewey asked her to marry him six months later, there didn't seem to be any other choice, she had to feed her family.

Elaine Littau

He had been so different from Pa. Of course he knew that Mama didn't really love him and that he would never take Pa's place. He gave Mama more jobs to do. She was in charge of anything that had to do with the house, and he did his work at the mill. There was little money, so any job to be done had to be done by Mama. She fixed the roof and chopped wood.

Nan was eleven when Pa died and hadn't appeared to grow much since. She was now fifteen and Elmer would soon be six; no one would have guessed her age. Mr. Dewy was determined to have a son. Mama finally was able to carry a child to term, but was not able to survive the birth. She was so weakened by hard work and miscarriages that the little baby brother was born dead. Nan was frightened for Elmer at that time because Mr. Dewey was annoyed with everything he did. One month later Mr. Dewey brought home a new wife. He never said where she came from only that they were to call her "Ma."

It was so hard to call a stranger Ma. They didn't know her name and she slapped them if they called her Mrs. Dewey. She became Ma. It seemed odd to say the word and have it only mean a label for someone in her life. No warm connections were attached to the word. Nan wondered how much Elmer remembered about Mama since he was pretty young when she went to heaven.

Heaven, Mama talked about heaven; she said that was where Pa was. Nan wished that she and Elmer could ride old Molasses to heaven. Maybe Mama would be singing there. Nan's eyes became so heavy; she could not hold them open. She drifted off as when remembered about her Mama telling her long ago about a stairway to heaven with angels going up and down. Maybe Molasses could find it and take them to Mama and Pa.

Chapter Three

Nan jerked awake just before she lost balance and fell off the back of the big horse. It was still pretty dark and she could barely make out the trees on the horizon. They came to a large clearing. Town was a half a mile to the north and the road continued westward, but Nan knew they couldn't go through the town and head north because someone might see them and tell Mrs. Dewey.

Elmer stirred in his sleep and Nan repositioned him to lie across her. The movement broke open some of the welts and she could feel her undershirt getting slightly wet. "Oh God, please make the bleeding stop. I can't get anything else and people would tell on me if they knew I'd been whipped." The bleeding stopped and the travelers rode on. At daybreak they came upon a stream and Nan pulled Molasses to a stop. She nudged Elmer and eased him to the ground. Gingerly she climbed off the very tall horse and grabbed the bedrolls.

Fumbling through the blankets she found the knotted handkerchief and pulled out the hard biscuit. "Elmer, we will have to share this. It will be our breakfast today." She tore the biscuit in half and gave Elmer his share. She found her tin cup and got some water from the stream and brought it to Elmer.

"Nan, I'm tired. Where are we going? Will Ma beat you again when she sees us?"

"Elmer, we are going away. I don't know where, but we must go fast so Ma will never see us again. Elmer, can you be brave and ride some more?"

"Yep, I don't want Ma beatin' you again." Nan rolled up the blankets and decided to have the beans for dinner or supper. They would have to do something else after that if they were going to eat again. There was nothing else left.

Elaine Littau

As they slowly traveled down the road, Nan began to think. Mrs. Dewey would be asking around if anyone had seen them. People would be looking for a girl and her little brother. She had to think of something. Just then they passed a small house next to the road. Elmer pointed and said, "Look, Nan, some woman left part of the wash on the line. Boy, wouldn't Ma skin us alive if we had done that!"

Nan blinked through the semi-darkness and saw a clothesline. Nan jumped off the horse and grabbed the clothes off the line. They smelled awful, like skunk, but she took them anyway.

"Now you know why they were on the clothesline, Elmer. Some boy got sprayed by a skunk and was trying to get them aired out before he washed them."

"Why did you take them, Nan?" questioned Elmer.

"Well, I need a disguise. They won't be looking for two boys," said Nan.

"Yep, but you would still look like a girl, you got long hair!"

"Elmer, do you have your pocket knife?"

"Yep."

"Let me see it."

"Okay."

Nan grabbed the little pocketknife and began sawing off first one black braid and then the other. Her hair was the same length as Elmer's. Nan sadly looked at the long braids in her hands, wrapped them in her old dress, and tied it to the bedroll. She then tugged on the loose fitting trousers and heavy shirt.

"Nan, you look just like a boy!" squealed Elmer.

"Let's cut us a couple of limbs and rig us up some fishing poles. If anybody sees us, they will think we are boys off fishing." Nan said. "You will have to call me another name. No boy would be called Nan. What shall it be?"

"I like Ned," said Elmer.

"Ned it is, Elmer. I look kinda like a Ned, huh?"

Silently the two rode into the west with the sun rising on their backs, the world brightening up little by little. Nan wondered how mornings seem full of new beginnings. *That is what we have, a new beginning*, she thought. If only she could figure out what to do next. Elmer needed food. They stopped next to a stream and she got out the little tin cup of cold beans. They shared and ate slowly.

"Nan, does your back still hurt?'

"Yep, Elmer. Do you think you could help me clean up the blood? I'm afraid that when I start sweatin' the blood will come through to the new shirt."

"Nan, she beat you bad! You don't got much skin that ain't broke open!"

"Elmer, we had to leave, else she would have took the strap to you. I never want you to have this pain."

"Sister, how far away are we? Are they going to look for us?"

"I don't know. We gotta let the horse rest and eat some grass. Maybe we can catch a fish while we lay here by this creek and sleep. You are tired aren't you, honey?"

Elmer stretched out on the grass and was soon asleep. As Elmer slept, Nan noticed some berries on bushes close to the creek. She took the tin cup and filled it up. She dumped the berries into the hanky and refilled the cup. She took the old rag from home and dipped it in the stream. Washing the grime from her face and arms without soap was quite a task. She was exhausted and laid on the ground next to Elmer while Molasses grazed nearby.

After a while Nan woke up stiff and sore. She could hardly move, but she knew she must. She gasped as she looked over at her young brother. He was so pale. She placed the cool damp rag on his forehead as he slowly opened his eyes. "Elmer, what is it?"

"My head is bustin,' Nan. I can hardly see."

"Honey, I forgot that you suffered yesterday with your head hurting. What caused it? Do you know?"

"I don't know, I think I'm gonna be sick."

Nan tried to think of a plan. What could she do? She wrapped the rag around his head and helped him back on the horse. The sun was high now. They hadn't caught any fish, but

Elaine Littau

they did have the berries. After finishing off the berries their stomachs still had a gnawing hunger. Nan heard a sound in the distance. It was a train whistle. She had heard trains before, but was much too frightened to approach one. She had to get Elmer to safety and maybe even a doctor. A water tower stood next to the tracks about one hundred yards away. Nan knew that the train would stop there to take on water. She gathered up their meager possessions and helped Elmer up to Molasses' back. They made it to some bushes next to the tracks just as the train rounded a curve and came to a stop at the water tower. Hurriedly Nan and Elmer carried their bundles to a boxcar with its door partly open. Nan lifted the tyke up and climbed in after him. They held their breath until the train slowly began rolling into the sunset. They looked through the gaps between the boxcar boards and bid goodbye to their dear friend, Molasses, and left all that was familiar to them behind. Elmer and Nan spread the bedrolls out in a dark corner of the boxcar and slept a deep exhausted sleep. The rhythm and movement of the train was comforting to the youngsters. As she slept Nan dreamed that she was being rocked in the arms of her mother.

They awoke to the sound of grating brakes. Blinking sleep from her eyes, Nan grew accustomed to the dark. Elmer was still lying on the pallet. His eyes were glazed over with pain. The rag on his head had dried with the warmth of the fever.

"Here Elmer, have some more berries. It is very dark tonight. I think we have traveled pretty far. Ma won't be looking for us since we have come this far."

They froze as they heard voices approaching the boxcar. Nan motioned for Elmer to stay quiet.

"Mr. Blake, there is room for your crates in this boxcar. Just tell your boys to bring them over here."

Nan hid Elmer behind a couple of bales of hay and huddled down beside him. A couple of farm hands brought twenty crates into the boxcar, shut and locked the door. After they left, Nan crawled up to the crates and discovered they contained apples and three crates of chickens along with various other supplies. Nan reached through the cracks in the crates and fished out a few eggs and several apples. She couldn't cook the eggs, but she knew that Elmer needed nourishment. She got the tin cup and broke one egg open into it. Quickly she swallowed it. It was slimy, but the gnawing slowed in her stomach. She fixed one for Elmer and told him to drink. He didn't know what it was and he asked for more. She fixed another and gave it to him. Then she handed him an apple. He quit moaning after he finished the apple and fell into a deep sleep.

Nan hated taking things that didn't belong to her, but lately she had been stealing a lot, first the clothes and now this food. When was she ever going to act like herself? She felt her hair where it was all cut off. The shorter hair managed to get in her eyes and her ears were cold. The back of her neck was exposed and she felt extremely ugly. There she sat, a lonely little girl, hiding in a boxcar full of crates with a sick little boy, propelling down a railroad track farther and farther west.

Elaine Littau

Chapter Four

Mary Dewey awoke early. She had little patience with folks who slept past five o'clock. The children were raised on the farm and they knew the routine. The cows were milked, the eggs were gathered, and then the breakfast was prepared. Mary grunted as she recalled that she still hadn't gotten the wood brought up to the house. She had gotten so worked up when she started whipping Nan that she forgot the reason for the whipping. Mary grimaced. She didn't know what had come over her since she married Mr. Dewey. She resented the formality, but Sam wouldn't let her call him anything else in front of the children. That man certainly had a lot of rules! Sure, she was a spinster, and she suspected that Sam realized how desperate she had become since her thirtieth birthday. He told her that he had two stepchildren he was responsible for, and that she would be their new Ma. She wanted a family and a husband, so she agreed to marry a man that she didn't love.

She wasn't prepared for the home she would be in charge of. Instead of being a run down, dirty shanty with unkempt children, she saw a lovely farm house, lovingly decorated, simple, clean, and efficient. The children were beautiful. Nan was a dark haired, brown-eyed girl with a soft, thoughtful look about her. Elmer was a sweet-faced, blond haired boy. They didn't need her. Nan was young, but she cared for the house as one with experience. Mary had never understood how or where to start running a home, and the idea that a girl fifteen years old knew more in this area irked her. Sam expected Mary to run things. Everything she tried to change had been a disaster. She ruined clothes, burned food, and found it impossible to get the children to call her Ma. She had to hit them to get them to say it. They began to look at her in fear. *Good, at least they are minding me.* If they didn't, she would give them reason to fear her. She began with a couple of swats. They jumped as soon as she ordered them. She became alarmed as she remembered her reaction at the sight of blood on Nan's back. She had not been raised to cause injury. Why had she done this? When the blood began soaking through Nan's dress she had become angry about the effort it would take to get the stain out. In her frustration she began hitting Nan harder and harder with the strap. The release of anger felt good to her. She quit when the strap became too heavy for her to lift. Nan lay there barely able to get a breath. Mary grew sick at her stomach to think that she had done all the damage to the body lying at her feet. Mary had never been hit much before she married Sam. He looked harmless, but he certainly brought pain when he wanted to. Working at the mill made him strong and frustration made him mean. He had left three months ago to be with his dying mother, and Mary was relieved to see him leave. Maybe she could sort out her thoughts and actions while he was gone.

She opened the old trunk in the corner of the kitchen to see if Nan and Elmer had more clothes that she could make over for them. The photograph on the top of the items had an unusual effect on her. A beautiful family was smiling at her from the frame. Mother, Father, daughter and son in their Sunday best looked like something out of a dream. Mary had always envied families such as this. She had always felt like an outsider, as if she were outside the window of a house looking in to a warm room with a cozy fireplace and a family sitting around the room speaking with laughter and common happiness, and she was not invited in. True, her family had been a good family—hard working, educated, and clean, but they were not especially happy. They made little time for play, and her mother and father were not affectionate to their children. Praise was considered a flaw. Mary remembered asking her mother to forgive her once, and Mom told her that she didn't believe that she was sorry. She would have to prove that she was sorry by being good. Mary had been at a loss as to what to do. She never remembered her mother smiling at her. The face in the photo seemed to mock her and show her that she had never proved her love to her mother. At one time, this woman had everything that Mary had wanted out of life, a loving, handsome, husband two sweet children, and a real home. Sam was gone. His mother had lingered longer than he had planned, and Mary was becoming worried that he might never return. *Enough of this thinking, I must get things done!* Mary said to herself.

She walked into the kitchen and noticed the bedrolls were already up from in front of the stove. She walked out the door and looked around the yard. She walked across to the barn and found that the cow had not been milked. *Where were those children?* She would have to look for them of course. *Where could they be? They weren't in the chicken house either.* Mary ran into the kitchen and looked around. The torn, bloody dress was lying in the corner and the old work dress was gone. The bedrolls weren't in the spot that they were kept. *Had the children run away? They had taken so little with them; of course they had very little that belonged to them. What should she do? What was she expected to do? What would Sam say?* Just at that moment she heard someone coming onto the porch.

Chapter Five

The sun was spilling a rosy glow across the sagebrush when Nan blinked her eyes open after hours of deep sleep. She could see the sunrise through the cracks in the boxcar. Elmer was still sleeping and Nan placed her hand on his brow. The fever had left. Maybe the headache that was tormenting him for the past three days had run its course. She smiled as she looked at his little boy face. He was a tough little guy. He never complained until things were unbearable. She was so proud of him. He still had a babyish look when he slept. His soft little cheeks and rosebud lips parted as he breathed. Mama had called him her "little golden boy;" Pa must have looked just like him at this age.

The chickens were clucking and flapping in their crates. Nan grimaced at the thought of more raw eggs, but she retrieved them and drank them down. Apples helped get the taste out of her mouth. She prepared some for Elmer. He sat up and looked into the tin cup. "Raw eggs, Nan?"

"Yep, go ahead, you had some last night.'

"Oh." He drank it down quickly and gnawed hungrily on the apple she handed him. "Where do you think we are, sister?"

Nan looked through the cracks of the boxcar and noticed dark blue mountains in the far distance. In the west there was desert-like land next to the train track up to the mountains and closer snow-capped mountains to the North. "I don't really know, but there will be a town soon."

"What town are we going to?" Elmer asked.

"I don't know, but Mama used to say to ask God for help and I think we should try to ask."

"Nan, I think God helped us already."

"Yes. Is your head better today?" Nan asked.

"Yes, I prayed and asked God to help it, and I asked Him for food and sleep, and to get away quick." Elmer smiled at the thought of his own prayers being answered so quickly.

"Just when did you do all this praying, Elmer?"

"All the time. Jesus is my friend. Mama said He walks with me, so I just tell Him what I'm thinking and He knows what I need. I prayed for you when you were getting whipped too."

"Do you think He cares about that?" Nan frowned.

"I know He does, and look! We got away fast and had eggs and everything. Right?"

"Mama told me about Jesus too. I guess I've been too sad about her dying and stuff to think He cares much about me." Nan quickly brushed a tear away.

"Nan, He does care…doesn't He? I need Him to care."

"Mama said He does, but I don't really know if He does. Why would he give us such bad trouble as we have had if He really cares?"

Elmer looked at her with a determined look in his five-year-old eyes, "I think He does care." His eyes were filled with tears. He looked so pitiful and sweet, but Nan wasn't very sure about whether God wanted to help them with everything that Elmer was asking for. Maybe He would help a little. That was all they needed now, just a little help.

"I guess it won't hurt us to ask for a little help," she grunted.

The train lurched to a stop. Nan saw hundreds of sheep next to the train. She heard shouts from the engineer and sheepherders. The engineer was angry about the sheep crossing the track. Elmer's eyes widened as he saw the sheepherder's dog running this way and that, moving the sheep across the tracks quickly. He sprang back and routed out stray sheep that were going the wrong way. He worked quickly and efficiently.

"Look Nan, that dog is moving as if he is having fun!"

Nan was amazed at the grace and agility of the humble little creature. She thought again, "humble" wasn't quite the word. She had never seen a dog trained for such a task. It was like watching a dance.

The train slowly began to roll. Nan and Elmer edged to the opposite side of the boxcar to watch the little dog as long as they could. There were two sheepherders, all those sheep, and one little black and white dog. When he disappeared from sight, they both were in their own thoughts. "That surely was a smart dog, Elmer."

"Do ya think we could ever get one, Nan, for our very own?"

"Well, we don't have any sheep...I don't know."

"Maybe we will get some sheep so we can have a little dog like that one."

Nan had no idea about sheep. How to get them, raise them, shear them, or anything. *Did you have to have a lot of land?* She just smiled and thought about that intelligent little dog. Nan began to plan. *Soon the train will stop, the door will be unlocked and we could get out. What will we do then? I must find a way to earn some money for food.* If she could only think of something she could do. Maybe chop wood or hoe in a garden or do other chores?

The train stopped on the edge of a fair-sized town. Nan watched as several men approached the boxcar. One of the fellows was short and stout with a mass of red hair and freckles. The second man was tall and lean with balding black hair. The third person was a big young boy with a sunburned face and blonde hair. The first unlocked the boxcar door and the three of them unloaded all the crates from the boxcar. After it was unloaded, the children climbed out of their hiding place behind the hay bales. The door was left open so Nan jumped to the ground. Elmer threw the bedrolls down to her and reached out for help to the ground.

Nan tied a bedroll to Elmer's back and one to her own. They kept the fishing poles and still had the look of two boys off fishing. Slowly they walked away from the train and over to the railroad station. There were a few men and boys milling around. Some of them were unloading freight.

"Hey, anyone, I need some help unloading these three box-cars! Any takers?"

Nan stepped up, "I'll do it!"

"Say boy, you're kind of a runt aren't you?"

"I'm strong." Nan stated.

"What's your name, kid?"

"Ned."

"Alright kid, see if you can unload that boxcar over there. There's fifty cents in it if you do a quick job of it. Pile the crates on this spot on the platform."

"Elmer, you sit over there under the tree and rest. We're gonna eat a good meal today!"

Nan lifted and stacked the crates one by one onto the platform. Some of them were heavy and others felt as if they had nothing in them. Most had labels: cloth, ammunition, crackers, or nails.

As Nan placed the last box on the platform, the small elderly man spoke to her, "Looks like you have managed to unload my shipment, young man. How would you like to help put all this on the shelves of my dry goods store and sweep up for me?"

"I would love to, sir," Nan answered quickly, "but I must feed my little brother first. Do you have a buckboard for me to load the crates onto?"

"So that little feller is your kid brother huh? Naw, don't bother about the buckboard; Lenny and Matt can deliver the crates to the store. As far as feed…Mama has dinner ready for me when I get there and she always makes too much for just me to eat. Come with me."

Nan called to Elmer and he ran over to her and the older man.

Chapter Six

Nate and Martha watched the hungry children devour more food than they could imagine. They ate very slowly and deliberately, relishing each mouthful. These little beggars were different than most runaways who had been fed in this kitchen. They had a real upbringing and manners. They were so grateful. Nate felt a knot forming in his stomach. Ned, the bigger one, was so concerned about the younger brother and was especially careful that he drank plenty of milk. Martha asked. "Ned, is the little one feeling sickly or something?"

"Yes, he suffers from blinding headaches. He hasn't had one today, but yesterday he hurt bad."

"Where are your kin?" Martha asked.

"Oh, at home. We jumped on the train for an exciting ride after we finished fishin,' but the people who loaded the boxcar, locked it, and we couldn't jump off like we planned. Ma is used to us getting carried away and havin' to spend the night out campin'…only…we forgot to pack a lunch…I guess we figured we'd catch a little more fish, but no luck."

Elmer looked at Nan and wondered how she could come up with such a big story so quickly. Nan was surprised herself! She had come up with some of it while unloading the boxcar. The rest just came out. She would have to remember exactly what she had said.

"Well, when you finish tidying up the store, I'll drive you home in the buckboard," Nate declared.

"Oh, we can walk," Nan responded quickly.

"We will see after the job is done," said Nate. Martha began clearing the dishes from the table. Nan and Elmer took their plates to the washbasin and started the dishwater as if by habit. Martha looked at the little ragged children in wonder, "Boys, I can do this, you look all done in."

Elmer grinned at her and said, "You're a nice lady. You cook good, too!"

"We really don't mind doing the dishes Mrs.—I'm sorry, I don't know your name," Nan smiled sweetly.

"Young. This is Nate Young and I'm Martha. You may find it funny that a couple so old would have the name of Young"

"Mama, we will forever be young because of it—isn't that right, boys!" Nate chortled.

"Elmer, you can stay with me while your brother goes to the mercantile to help Nate stock the shelves. That would be okay wouldn't it be, Ned?" Martha winked at Nan.

⁂

Nan and Nate worked on stocking the shelves for the better part of the afternoon. Nan began sweating profusely and became weak as she tried to earn the wonderful dinner they had just eaten. Once she began to fall from the ladder leaned against the tall shelves. Nate put his hand on her back to brace her. She almost cried out. The look of pain in her eyes and the pink sweat all across the back of her shirt did not escape Nate's eyes. It was then that Nate spoke, "Ned, boy, lets save the rest of this work for tomorrow. Here is a cup of water. You look as if you need it."

Nan drank thirstily from the cup and began to worry when she looked up and saw Nate studying her face.

"Boy, I know you are a runaway. You are hurt bad. Your shirt is starting to soak with blood." At this Nan jumped up and started to get ready to run, only Elmer was still with Mrs. Young.

"This is the truth isn't it, boy?"

"Yes sir."

"Let me put some salve on your back and while I'm cleaning you up, you can tell me what is going on." Nate went to the cupboard where he kept the salves and ointments.

"Take off your shirt and I'll doctor you up."

Nan pulled the shirt carefully from her back and held the bloody and sweaty, skunk scented rags close to her chest.

"I have never seen anything so..."

Nate couldn't continue. Tears caught in his throat, "I better get the doc."

Nan jumped up, "No! Please don't! I don't want anyone else to know!"

"Little feller, there is really angry cuts, puss, and bruises. Your skin is so hot, you have fever and it might get worse. Who did this to you?"

"I can't tell you," Nan said, quietly.

"Your Ma or Pa?"

"No, they would never beat me like this!"

"Well somebody did something! I will get the sheriff if you don't tell."

"Please don't! It was my step-ma! I can't let Elmer go back there. She was gonna start on him next!"

"I don't know what to do. I do know that I'll not take you back to any person who would cut up a kid like this! Martha will know what to do." Tears ran down Martha's face as she looked at Nan's back. She had never seen such a mess. "Ned, you said that you got this whippin' so your brother wouldn't get it."

"Yes ma'am, It really was my fault for not getting the firewood."

"Did you know, a long time ago a young man took a bad beating so that we could be healed by God. He was the Son of God."

Elmer came across the room and stood close to Nan.

She continued. "Yes, just before he was crucified on a cross. He was beaten. The Scripture says, 'He was wounded for our transgressions. He was bruised for our iniquities and by His stripes we are healed."

"What does that mean?" asked Elmer.

"It means that He died on the cross for our sin and He was beaten so that we can be healed. Honey, I'm going to pray

Elaine Littau

for you while I put some more of this salve on you." Martha prayed a fine, simple prayer as she carefully administered to the broken flesh. "Now you must get into some fresh clothes and rest in bed. You are quite feverish."

"Ned, come here."

Nan had forgotten her new name and failed to respond. Elmer chimed in, "Nan, Martha wants you to follow her to the bedroom."

"Nan, is it? Dear me, a little girl? What is wrong, dearie?

Nan blanched. She saw Mr. Dewey walking down the street past the Young's house. Everything went black.

Chapter Seven

Nan awoke the next morning in puzzlement. Elmer was snuggled next to her in a real bed. It was soft and warm. She felt fresh and clean. She could barely remember what it felt like to be so clean. She gazed at Elmer as he slept. He looked so good! He had been tired for so long and now he truly looked relaxed. Nan smiled as she thought of the nice couple who had fed them and let them sleep in this wonderful bed. A cloud slipped over Nan's face as she remembered she had seen Mr. Dewey walking around in this very town! She mustered up strength enough to get out of bed, but found weakness holding her down. She would have to speak to Elmer about what they had to do next. As long as they stayed inside they would be all right. She would rest and let Elmer rest too, and in a day or two they would be strong enough to leave.

She let her imagination go as she thought of having a home like this to live in forever, but it couldn't be. Mr. Dewey was here. They had to leave. The Youngs would never stand for them just leaving, so they must run away, again. Martha stood in the door and watched Nan as she laid thinking in her bed. *Poor child! The pain some people inflict on mere children.* Martha noticed the nervous look on Nan's face. She knew Nan didn't feel safe from her stepmother yet, and she knew Nan would need to leave before too long.

With this in mind Martha went to the breakfast table to talk with Nate as he took breakfast. Nate was enjoying his bacon and pancakes. He gulped a swallow of hot coffee when Martha approached him with a question, "Nate, can you think of any place those children could go where they could feel safe?"

What is wrong with here?" Nate asked.

"Nan doesn't feel safe here?"

"How would you know that?" he asked, puzzled.

"Just a look I saw on her face."

"We'll, just tell her she's okay here."

"No, we don't want them running away again...landing who knows where. We need to think of something." Martha began to wring her hands.

"It is too bad Fred isn't here to think of something, Mama"

"Fred! You know that is a great idea!"

"What? Nate asked.

"We can send them to his house!"

"Do you think that would be wise?" Nate's eyebrows shot up.

"Why not, who would think of looking for them at Fred's house?"

"You mean cabin?" He rubbed the stubble on his chin.

"Yes, cabin, but he lives in the wilderness and no one would look there." Martha said with satisfaction.

"Let's tell the children." Nate said.

Nan could hardly believe her ears that Martha and Nate understood she and Elmer couldn't stay here even without her saying anything. What's more, Nate was taking them to their son's house in the wilderness of Colorado, a mountain place close to the mining town of Silverton. Mrs. Dewey would never look for them there.

After two weeks of rest, Nate bundled the two up and placed them on a couple of pack mules loaded down with supplies. There was enough to see them through the winter. Nan and Elmer were quite strong now; it had been ten days since Elmer's last headache. It had been a long time since Nan had felt so well cared for, and tears flowed down her cheeks as she told Martha goodbye. Martha promised her that Fred would bring them back for a visit someday or that she would come see them in the spring.

The landscape was beautiful as well as treacherous, but with Nate's skillful maneuvering they arrived at the cabin in a week. Fred stepped out of his cabin as Rufus, his husky, barked an alarm.

"Hey Rufus, its Grandpa, don't be hollering at me!" laughed Nate.

"Papa, what are you doing here!" cried Fred.

"I brought you some supplies and company for the winter." The grin on Nate's face faded as he saw the pained expression on his son's face.

"Pa, what were you thinking? This ain't a place for younguns!"

"Son, these little soldiers need a safe place to hide for a spell."

"What have you gotten me into?" Fred asked.

Nan heard the exchange and fear gripped her. She hadn't thought Fred might be different than Nate and Martha. *Why hadn't they just run off on their own?* She held her head high and spoke quietly and with authority. "If we are not welcome, we surely shall not be staying. We can fend for ourselves."

Nate watched his son as Nan spoke to him. "Boy, I don't know you, but if you and the youngun over their need to winter here, you can."

"Fred, she's a little girl, not a boy, it is a disguise she came up with," said Nate.

Fred blushed and asked, "Pa, how do you expect me to take care of a girl and a little boy when I couldn't even take care of my own?"

"You have been blaming yourself too long; you need these kids as much as they need you."

"Pa, do you think any girl can survive the winters here?" Fred asked.

"Freddy, all I know is that if Nan gets discovered by her stepmother, she wouldn't survive another beating like the last one."

"Beating? No! I'm sorry!"

"It isn't your problem, mister. I can take care of my brother and myself!"

"Nan, you can stay here," Fred said firmly.

"We will earn our keep and not be a burden to you then."

"Sounds fair to me, son," said Nate.

"I was fixing beans and cornbread. There is plenty..." Fred's voice trailed off.

"Let's eat!" cried Elmer who as of yet had said nothing.

The beans were delicious! As Nan spooned some of the bean broth between her lips she looked around the room. It was a rough log cabin. It was much rougher than her girlhood home, but there was a cozy quality to the room. The meal had been prepared in the huge fireplace. Fred had two Dutch ovens placed in the coals. One was for the beans, and the other for cornbread. The packs from the mules stood in the far corner. Nan's eyes traveled around the room. Fred had a huge featherbed. *Imagine that!* At the foot of the bed, piled with blankets and clothing and other supplies, was a small trundle bed. It was odd for a mountain man to have a feather bed and then odder still for him to have this other bed, too. Fred saw her looking around and studying the room with a questioning look.

"That bed belonged to my little girl, Joy. She and my wife, Claire, died with influenza last winter."

"Oh," was all Nan could say. That explained a lot.

"Fred, let me help you put away the supplies now and then we should all get to bed. I'll be going home at first light."

Nan and Elmer watched the horizon until the last traces of their friend Nate had disappeared. He and Martha were good to them. Finally they were safe from "Ma." As they turned and faced the crude cabin, Nan couldn't help but wonder about the man that they were "wintering" with and how they would fare under his care. She did not want charity, but she was smart enough to know that there was no way that she and Elmer could earn their keep. She resolved to do what she could. Entering the room she saw a bucket next to the door and grabbed it, telling Elmer that she was going to the creek for water to do the breakfast dishes.

She spied the creek and placed the bucket on edge to fill with the clear sparkling liquid. Taking a deep breath, the clear crisp air filled her lungs and renewed her energy. Cardinals were in the spruce tree making a nest. The sun was almost all the way up, and she loved the way the golden rays felt on her face. Maybe this place would be a good home after all. She lifted the bucket and carried it up to the cabin door. Fred saw her carrying the water trying not to slosh it as she walked. She had such a serious determined look about her that he couldn't help but be amused. It was evident that she was trying to work for their keep. *A young child like that shouldn't have those kinds of worries.* Fred smiled at her as he took the bucket. "What were you planning on doing today, little traveler? I do hope that you weren't planning on working on such a glorious day as this one promises to be."

"There are dishes to do!"

"Yes there are, but I will do them this time. You guys get some dinner things together and we will go fishing and have a picnic by the fishin' hole."

"What do you mean?"

"I mean that it is time you kids learned to have some fun."

Chapter Eight

The trout were delicious prepared over the open fire. They ate until they could hardly move. Nan enjoyed seeing the excitement and pleasure play across Elmer's face each time he caught a fish. His eyes were bright and the shine had come into his hair. He had put on some much needed weight. Nan leaned her back against a big aspen tree and realized that she could do so with no pain. The wounds were healed. She no longer ached in her joints and the bruises were gone. A pink glow had found her cheeks and she looked the picture of healthy girlhood. The fishin' hole had become a dinnertime ritual in the weeks they had been with Fred. Fred was looking more peaceful and happy himself. They made a perfect little family.

Everyone had been working hard preparing for winter. Fred cut wood while Nan and Elmer stacked it close to the cabin—it would take a lot of firewood to get through the winter storms. Nate and Martha sent more than adequate provisions, and Fred was grateful they had so that he could have time to bring a little happiness into the lives of the children.

He educated them in the laws of the wilderness: tracking game, fishing, hunting and preserving the meat. All the meat was smoked and dried in the fashion of the nearby Indians. He showed them healing herbs and poisonous plants and how to care for their animals. They had a pack mule named Ruby, and then there was Rufus the dog, and the mustang stallion, Sonny. Fred was amazed at how quickly they learned. He discovered that they had very little formal schooling, so he promised them that in the winter months, he would teach them how to read and write and do sums. He decided that it was good for him to move past the pain of losing his wife and child to help these children with getting past their pain.

Nan's favorite place was the stream. As she sat there, she knew that she had never been as safe and happy since her parents died. The sound of the water splashing against the rocks and the lush meadow toward the cabin spoke to her of peace. She knew that Elmer was happy too. Happiness was such a wonderful emotion. Fear, torment and anger all seemed so far away. Fred was kind like his Ma and Pa. He hadn't laid a strap to them yet. Of course, they were careful to mind him. He was human, and humans get angry and hurt those who aggravate them. Nan knew this well. She also knew that if he started in on them that they would just move on, after winter.

The days were short and the sun was slipping behind the mountain peak. Nan shivered as she hurried down the path to the cabin. Inside, she smelled the welcome aroma of beans and cornbread. She had learned how to put the beans on to cook in the morning so that by supper they would be ready. Fred had cooked the cornbread. Nan was still amazed that a man would actually put his hand to cooking, but she guessed Fred was used to fending for himself and wanted the cornbread to be done so they could eat sooner.

Everything tasted great! Of course they had to wait while Fred asked the blessing. Nan knew where the food came from, and she didn't see that God did much to get it to their table, but if Fred wanted to say a prayer, it was fine with her. She and Elmer cleaned up the dishes after supper and Fred began to read to them from his wife's Holy Bible. Some of the words were vaguely familiar to Nan, but it had been years since she had heard them from her mother's lips. She and Elmer had cried when they heard Fred read about Adam and Eve having to leave the Garden of Eden. Nan thought about how awful it would be to leave this beautiful Colorado wilderness. Fred had to explain to them that even though Adam and Eve left the garden, God still loved them and was taking care of them.

Elaine Littau

Tonight they would be reading about Joseph. He seemed a lot like Elmer to Nan. They hurried so that the reading could begin. Before they started though, this time, Fred had them sit at the table. He gave them a broken piece of flat stone called slate and a crumbly white rock. He showed Elmer how to write his name on the slate. He loved knowing what his name looked like. He tried several times and Fred told him it wouldn't take many times of practice before he would learn it. Then the reading began. Fred told them that the Bible was written thousands of years ago. Nan just couldn't believe that something so old could be so interesting. After the reading came the memory work. Fred was teaching them the twenty third Psalms and the Lord's Prayer; the words were beautiful and powerful. Nan didn't understand the meaning of some of the words, and she knew that Elmer didn't either, but it made her happy to think of herself as a fluffy white lamb and God taking care of her. One day Nan asked Fred, "What does hallowed mean?"

"Holy I think."

"Oh" Nan frowned, "What exactly is holy?"

"Without sin."

"What are trespasses?"

"Sins."

"Oh. I don't think I have tres—sinned against anyone, but they sure have sinned against me!"

Fred's eyes looked amused, "Is that right?"

"I don't want to forgive my stepma for everything she did to us."

Fred looked concerned. "Well, Nan, the *want to* has to come from God. Remember, Joseph forgave his brothers for selling him to the slave traders in our last Bible reading. God had to help him do that."

"I never cared for my stepmother and I never want to see her again, and I enjoy hating her!"

"Nan, hate is a disease that will destroy you. When you forgive those who sin against you, God will help you from falling into temptation and deliver you from evil. It is God's power that does this."

"I'm not ready to let go of the hate!" Nan was crying hard and clenching her fists. "I guess God can't love me if I want to hate people!"

"That's not true, Nan. The Bible says, 'Yea, I have loved you with an everlasting love that while you were yet sinners, Christ died for you.'"

"I will have to think on that a while. I don't know what I want to do. Maybe I better not say The Lord's Prayer until I figure it all out. I am not a liar." With that said, she went to the trundle bed and lay beside Elmer who was sleeping peacefully.

Fred watched her as he pretended to read. Nan was usually so sweet and gentle. He had rarely seen this hate filled side of her. Her anger had been strong, real and justified, but it was not good for her. He knew what she was going through because he had been angry with God about Claire and Joy's deaths. There were still times when he wanted to scream out his "whys?" to God. These children had unknowingly shown him that life must go on even when terrible things have happened. He would never be able to explain to them how a loving God could let their Mama and Papa die leaving them with the cruel caretakers, or why the girl he loved since childhood and their playful little daughter, Joy, had been snatched away by the stealthy blow of influenza. *Were there answers? Had he forgiven and was he forgiven? Had he forgiven his previous "flock" for their unjust behavior?* He spent the better part of the night in prayer, and when he laid on the featherbed that night his soul was at peace with the Holy Father in heaven.

Elaine Littau

Chapter Nine

Mary knew the man who was knocking loudly on her door. He was a nosey sort that seemed to always poke around their place to "check on the younguns."

"I'm comin', Jeb. Can I help ya?"

"Your old Molasses was wandering by the train tracks this morning and I wondered if them kids had let him out or what? The gate was closed."

"They probably went fishing. You know kids, Jeb, they like to play all they can."

Jeb looked past her into the room. "Well he's in the pasture now. Tell Nan and Elmer howdy for me. Say, when is Sam comin' home?"

"Directly. I don't want to keep you from your work. Bye now." Mary shut the door a little too firmly to be neighborly, but Jeb was just snooping. *I ain't lettin' nobody know 'bout them kids. I'll have to come up with something if Jeb comes back though. Let's see...They can't be fishin' forever! Do they have any kin somewhere, anywhere? I jist as well make up some kinfolk that they might go to visit. It would be fittin for them to see kin. Think, old gal...They went to an aunt's house, yeah a great Aunt...Gracie in Boston. I'll tell Sam that too. Maybe he will be glad to be rid of them. I'll tell him Aunt Gracie gave us the house and land since she is so rich and we won't divide inheritance with the kids. That will make him happy.*

She scurried around the house and removed every trace of the children, putting everything into the trunk. Struggling, she put the trunk into the buckboard, hitched up Molasses and took the trunk to the old train station. As the stationmaster greeted the sweating, agitated, Mary Dewey, he noticed the large trunk on the buckboard. "I need to send this trunk to Boston and I need two tickets to Boston for the children.

Uh, they are on the train already and I will take the tickets to them."

"They will have to change trains three times. Are you certain you shouldn't get a ticket and go with them?" The old clerk asked.

Mary thought for a moment, she could go and escape everything, but what would she do in Boston? She had a home now and husband, maybe. She had more of a chance with Mr. Dewey than some unknown person that may never come along. "No, Nan is fifteen and she is smart. They will do fine."

"Address to send the trunk to?"

"None. Their great aunt will arrange that when they get there. She may not even claim it after they get there. She doesn't want anything from us. She is quite wealthy you know. Uppity if you must know. Afraid we weren't giving them culture and stuff. Those people just ain't grateful to us...except they did give us the farm." Mary could hardly believe that she was telling all these lies to this complete stranger. Truthfully, she never wanted to see those kids again and she would have to figure out what to do if they ever did come back. She would figure that out when and if it happened. She took the tickets and headed for the passenger car, walked in and through a couple of cars, then got on the platform and waved to her non-existent charges. She was very proud of her creativity in this expensive lie. It was expensive, but worth it.

The scorching day was bearing hard on Mary's back as she drove the old horse into the farmyard. The place was still neat and orderly, but there was something strangely quiet about it. She had Molasses take the buckboard to the lean-to shed next to the barn, and then she unharnessed the gentle workhorse and led him out to the pasture. She gave a sigh as she watched the animal nibble the grass. Life was lonely. That was a hard fact that Mary just had to live with. The children had always spoken in soft tones to one another when they were settling down for the night. It had been a pleasant sound even if it did smite her in her heart that she never would be that close to anyone. One day, if she had a child of her own, she would speak softly. The child would want to wrap chubby little arms around her and call her Mama. The glow of love would shine in baby eyes. Never would she lay a hand on a child again. *I swear it! I don't know what got into me. I am not a monster without feelings. I can be good. I will myself to change. I am starting today!* Now that Nan and Elmer were gone, she had a new start. No one would remember the harsh treatment and words. She could do it. *Turning over a new leaf, right. Other people could do it, why not me. I am going to be so good that people will talk about me. I will make friends. I don't like being alone on this vast prairie. I must have someone to talk to.*

Now that she made that commitment to herself, how would she go about carrying it out? *Where do I start?* It used to be that acquaintances were made while going to school. *I am too old for school. I will go into town tomorrow and get some things in the general store. I will speak to the lady at the counter. I better start slow, I don't want people to notice too much of a change in me. I will ask her a question about herself. It shouldn't be too personal. What do other people talk about? Weather. Let me see. "Mrs. Waide, it is mighty hot weather we have been having lately." I should say something about Nan and Elmer. Let me see…"I am sure that my children, Nan and Elmer, are enjoying their visit with their aunt in Boston." What will I say if they ask how I could let them stay or live there? Nancy, the children's mother, had an elderly aunt that truly wanted to raise the children herself. There are a lot of other cousins that would add a wonderful influence in their lives. That's it. I need to look like I am doing it for the good of the children. I will say that a little bit. "…for the good of the children." That sounds mighty kind of me. I can tell how lonesome it was for them out on the little farm and how much culture they will get in the big city. I can even say that I miss the big city. I know, I'll say that I love the shopping and theatre and miss it so much. That might make me sound more interesting. It is a sight better than the truth. I need to get my story straight.*

She walked slowly to the house and looked at the clothes on the hooks in her room. There wasn't much, but there was a dress her mother helped her make for her wedding. It was no more that a fancier version of her work dresses, but she had been saving it for a special occasion. Well, this was a special occasion. She was making a brand new Mary Dewey. Maybe she would have enough egg money to buy some fabric for a new dress. At the very least, she did need some more chicken feed. That would mean that she could get feed sacks in a pretty print. The fabric was coarse, but some of it was kind of pretty. She would have to get at least three sacks, probably four to make it look like anything. Mr. Dewey would have a fit if she bought that much at one time, but he wasn't here now, was he?

She looked into the mirror over the washbasin by the door. Good folk wouldn't welcome a woman that looked so severe. *"If I'm going to make myself over, then I need to do it right!"* She took down the braids that were wrapped tightly around her head and unwound them. She had good hair. Not wonderful like the mother of the children, but she might try to do something with it. She better not be too different though. If Mr. Dewey showed up, it wouldn't do for him to notice a change all at once. She thought of the photograph in the trunk that she had sent to Boston. Mary had her hair technically fashioned in the same manner that Nancy wore hers. There was a difference though. Nancy wove the strands a little looser than Mary liked hers to be. It gave a softer look to the hair. Mary liked hers to be tight and smooth so that none of it would ever dare escape during a day of hard work. She had to remind herself that she was reinventing herself. *Softer, looser, not so tight...*After a few attempts, she managed to mimic Nancy's style perfectly.

There was something still wrong. There was no light in her eyes. "Love light" she heard a busybody woman say at a wedding in her hometown. Well, she had no love light. Did she love anyone? Mary paused for a few moments to reflect on her life. Was there no one that could cause her to have love light in her eyes? After some intense thinking, Mary finally thought of someone. Yes, there was someone, the child that she would have someday. She thought of the child and looked in the mirror. Her eyes were somewhat warmer, but pain and trouble were mingled in with the new warmth of love.

She got out the old wooden ironing board and flat irons. After stoking the fire in the wood stove, she finally got the flat irons hot. She worked on smoothing the wrinkles out of the tired fabric until the first flat iron grew cold. She then proceeded to work with the second flat iron while the first one reheated on the stove. It was a long, tiring process, but she just had to look her best. Maybe she needed to look better than her best.

Chapter Ten

Winter would be coming on in a few weeks, and signs of the change of season were everywhere. The aspen had put on their yellow coats and stood watch over the meadow, and Nan and Elmer were growing bronze and healthy with all the fresh air and good food. It was so beautiful here that Nan could almost forget the past. She had taken a few clothes to the stream to wash when she heard a noise in the trees. It was men's voices. She scurried to the tall brush and hid. They were talking loudly and their laughter boomed in the quiet meadow. There were three of them. They looked to be trappers with pelts laid across the back of a pack mule. They were anticipating the celebration they would have after the sale of their pelts. Nan trembled and hoped that she would not be discovered. Fred had gone out to check his trap lines and Elmer had gone with him with Rufus trailing along. She never anticipated seeing another human being while they were gone. She listened to their banter as they let their horses drink from the stream. Hopefully they would not spy the wet clothes lying close to the bank. As they looked toward the cabin the tallest of the three spoke, "I reckon ole Fred wouldn't mind if we got us a little grub."

"Probably not."

They seemed to be in agreement. They strode up to the cabin and opened the latch and let themselves in.

"Man oh man, this boy is stocked up!"

"Good, then it won't run him short if we eat," said the toughest looking one of the bunch. They stayed in the cabin for such a long time that Nan's legs were numb. She couldn't have moved if she had wanted to. Eventually they left the cabin and got on their horses with the pack mule in tow.

"Seemed like an excess of plates out to me, Sam. What do you think?"

"Maybe Fred got hisself a squaw."

"Maybe."

"He beats all I ever seen. Keepin' to hisself all this time and now a squaw. Wonder if he reads that Bible to her."

They roared with laughter most of the way down the mountain. The last intelligible words Nan heard was, "Imagine that, a Christian injun woman! He's quite the gent alright."

Nan pulled her legs out from under her and waited for the painful tingle to hit them. She was so relieved to finally get out from the bushes. Stretching, she listened for their voices and heard nothing except the rush of the stream. Clumsily, she approached the cabin. They used quite a few supplies, but at least they were gone. She wondered where the dirty plates were, but realized after viewing the table that they hadn't used any. There were few crumbs, signs of a meal eaten off the table. She was glad that the trundle bed was put under the big one so the men wouldn't know that there might be more than one new person living with Fred. She wiped off the table and used the makeshift broom to clean up the floor. She had learned from Fred how to sweep a dirt floor to make it clean. He had showed her to sprinkle water on the dirt and then sweep lightly. The loose dirt would sweep away leaving a hard packed dirt surface. He said that his wife, Claire, was just beginning to crochet a rag rug when she died. Her plans had been to put the colorful rag rug on the hardened dirt floor to make the room cozier. Nan had never learned to crochet, but she had a nice rag rug at home. She had to agree with Claire, they did make a room cozy.

Without warning, tears were streaming down Nan's tanned cheeks at the thought of her home and mother. Mama had made such a wonderful home for her and Elmer and Dad. Why did it all have to end so soon? Nan could hardly remember the details of how her mother looked. Actually all she could remember was the photograph that Mr. Dewey had made Mama put in the big trunk the day they were married. Nan snuck in and looked at it whenever Mary Dewey was in town getting supplies. She and Elmer just stared at the happy family inside the four walls of the picture frame. Nan scolded herself, "Well, girl, quit crying. You are safe and Fred treats you and Elmer pretty fine."

"What's wrong, Nan" whispered Elmer as he looked into the cabin. Nan had left the door open and hadn't heard Fred and Elmer walk up. She jumped in alarm, afraid that the trappers had returned. "I was just thinking about how life has as many bends in it as a little mountain creek."

Elmer smiled, he liked the way Nan strung words together like a storybook. "I still don't know what you mean, but I hope it was happy thinking, sister."

Just then Fred ducked into the doorway. "How were things while we were gone, Nan?"

"Well, some trappers came by while I was at the creek and ate a good portion of our supply. I stayed hidden in the brush and didn't try to stop them."

"How many were there?"

"Three. A tall lanky man and a short red headed younger man and…"

"I know those men. They will leave us be. They probably went into Silverton to get some supplies and sell their pelts. They will probably stay on Blair Street until most of their money is spent on drink and…" Fred had forgotten that he was talking to naïve children and just let the words trail off. He knew that nothing good could come from hanging around Silverton's Blair Street. He had tried it when Claire and Joy died and their memory still refused to be blocked out.

Fred looked through the remaining supplies and mentally estimated the amount of food it would take to survive the winter. Elmer and Nan were sensible eaters and understood the need for discretion. Still, he made the decision to go hunting at first light tomorrow so that he could restore their meat supply and have time to get it made into jerky.

It was still dark when Fred got together his bedroll and food to take with him on his hunt. He would be gone for no less than three days. He knew he would be going up farther than his trap lines; the deer would be thick in the area that he was going for the hunt. He hoped to get a quick kill, dress the meat, and get back to cabin before the snow started falling. There was plenty of food for the children while he was gone, but he didn't know how they would get along without an adult to watch over them. Those trappers shouldn't be back by the place for a good three to four days and he would be back before then. Those scoundrels, they meant him no harm, but he knew that they could be trouble when they wanted to be.

The faithful dog was all keyed up to travel with him, but he looked back at the cabin. Duty toward the children beckoned him. "Rufus, why don't you stand guard over Nan and Elmer? They need you more than I do right now."

Reluctantly, Rufus walked to the cabin. It was all Fred could do to keep from chuckling at the obedient dog. He certainly had been a lifesaver to him. It was harder to leave him behind that he had at first thought. "Oh, grow up, Fred!" he said chastising himself.

Before too long the sun started shining on the other side of the mountain. The sky brightened a little and the pines stood as dark outlines against it. Sonny and Ruby knew the way to Fred's hunting grounds. Onward they went until the sun broke over the high mountain. It was strange to be alone in the woods again. He hadn't thought the presence of his visitors had really made that much difference in him. He knew that they were healing emotionally and physically. Boy, had they needed all that healing. Elmer had managed to go for ten to twelve days at a time without a headache. As Fred quietly picked his way up the trail, he wondered about the headaches. *Something isn't right about all that. Poor kid is only five years old; he shouldn't even know much about pain.* Nan said that he would be six in February. They would have to do something to make this birthday special for him.

Tracks. It looked to be about three deer, possibly a doe with two fawns. Well, he wouldn't leave the little ones orphans. More tracks appeared on the far side of the creek. These were larger, perhaps a buck. Fred would like to take aim on a large buck and keep his antlers for a souvenir. They would look handsome above his fireplace mantle. Just then he heard the snap of a twig. A magnificent buck walked into the clearing just in front of Fred. He hadn't caught scent of him, as Fred was downwind. Fred took careful aim and brought the animal down with the first shot. He ran to the buck and checked him to make certain that he was dead. He didn't want the animal to have any unwarranted suffering. Quickly, Fred began to dress the buck, putting the meat into several bundles. He walked back to the spot where Sonny and Ruby were standing and took them to retrieve the bundles of meat.

Just as he finished tying them onto the pack mule, a clap of thunder sounded through the forest. No sooner had the thunder boomed, than the rain began pouring from the heavens. Fred scanned his surroundings and spied a cave on the side of a mountain. He spurred the animals on to the natural shelter. The rain began to freeze as it continued to pound the earth. Sleet formed and soon turned into snow. The snow blew and swirled minute upon minute, hour upon hour. Fred shivered in the cold, damp cave. He brought the animals into the cave with him. It was good that it was big enough to accommodate the three of them. Fred plunged into the darkness and found a dead tree close to the mouth of the cave. It was wet, but he always carried some kindling with him on his pack for days on his hunt that all the wood was wet. He started with just a couple of small twigs and a good portion of his kindling. He got out his flint and proceeded in the ancient art of making a fire. After the first twigs started blazing, Fred added more twigs to the fire. Patiently he tended the fire and was rewarded with the warmth it provided as he finally was able to add small sticks, and eventually a good-sized branch to it. Fred then took the packs and saddle off the animals and gathered a good measure of snow to melt for water for them. Pa had taught him that eating too much snow would drop his body temperature too quickly and make it nigh to impossible to get warmed up. He figured the animals would appreciate the warm liquid as much as he would. He reached into his pack and found the feed that he had brought along. His father had instructed from childhood to take good care of the animals he owned and they would take good care of him. Fred smiled at the thought of how his father's voice sounded in the early mornings when he was teaching a young Fred the value of nurturing the beasts of burden. On more than one occasion he had given his friends the speech and mocked his father's voice. His friends had roared with laughter. Fred could sound exactly like his little father when he wanted to. The snow whipped around the spruce trees and showed no sign of letting up. He got out some of the provisions that he had packed and proceeded to make some coffee. The hot liquid would warm him. His clothes were starting to steam and become uncomfortable to him so he got out his bedroll and found the extra pants and shirt that he rolled in with the blanket. He made a makeshift tripod to hang his wet clothes on to dry by the fire. After drinking the coffee, Fred lay down to sleep. He would have to wake every quarter hour to feed the fire, but the warmth was worth it. It was bound to be a long night.

Fred awoke the next morning and the fire was nearly out. He stirred the embers into a small flame. He looked out the opening and the snow was still falling. He needed to get back to the cabin soon for the children, and for his own sanity. The same old memories flooded his consciousness. *No, I refuse to think about all that again!* Try as he would, the memories invaded. There was Claire and Joy in the cabin. They needed an escape from the vicious people who had made him doubt his calling into the ministry. He had brought them to live on the mountain to experience the beauty of the Rocky Mountains and God's creation. He thought that the good fresh air would be just the thing for them. He was using the year that they would spend there to be an intense search for God's will. The Bible was his meat and drink. God was his close Companion. One day a man had come to the cabin for help. He had a fever and desired prayer. He had a bluish tint to his skin and said that he felt as if he had been beaten all over. They tried to nurse him to health, but before they could even make out a bed for him, he died in Claire's arms. A few days later Joy came down with a fever and almost immediately afterwards it affected Claire too. They died in a matter of hours. They were too sick to move. The town had no doctor even if he got them there.

Fred had sat on the ground next to the fresh graves and waited for the influenza to attack him and put him out of his misery. Nothing happened. His Ma and Pa came out to check on the little family only to find him laying next to the graves in a mental stupor. They took him home with them and tried to bring his weary mind a little peace. He just couldn't stop crying. Finally, in a rage, he yelled at God and took off for Silverton and the wicked Blair Street. He spent months in the saloons and houses of ill repute in hopes to get the memories out of his mind. He was also running from God. The memory of that chapter in his life was one of the ghosts that Fred could never shake. He prayed about it, but he just couldn't leave the mountain and the two graves next to that confounded cabin. He felt so weak in his walk with God that the thought of ministering to anyone else was laughable. His thoughts turned to Nan and Elmer. Now here were two people who understood pain and the need for solitude. For as young as they were, they knew how to leave a man be if he needed to think. Fred felt as if he were looking at his eightieth year instead of the twenty-two actual years he had spent on the earth.

It had been good to laugh again. The kids had a great sense of humor and imagination. Fred smiled as he thought of the day in October that they had been fishing and lying on a blanket next to the stream watching the clouds. Elmer was so intent on finding objects in the clouds. Nan described doggies and faces to him and he stared with wide eyes. He said that he could see all that Nan pointed out and even more. Fred had enjoyed the make believe time with them. For a while, he was able to be like a kid. It felt so good.

Just then a gust of wind hit the interior of the cave. When was this blizzard going to let up? He was starting to worry about getting home to the kids. He was hoping that the snow wouldn't be as bad lower down the mountain at the cabin site. He picked up a stick and stirred the fire, and then he got some snow and melted it for coffee. Boy, he surely was lonely!

Chapter Eleven

Nan and Elmer had seen the storm clouds gathering and decided to bring a massive amount of firewood indoors. Fred had told them that it was important to have plenty inside and dry in case a sudden blizzard came upon them. He told them of instances that people would freeze to death trying to get back to the house from the barn. He had rigged up a clothes-line to run from the barn to the cabin for the winter so that they could feed the animals and find the way to the cabin by holding onto the line. Elmer had taken scraps to Rufus and asked Nan if Rufus could stay inside the cabin because of the approaching storm. Nan told him that they would let him in as soon as it hit. Rufus was much happier outside and hated being indoors. They had just sat down to a hot plate of beans when the three trappers banged on the door and let themselves in. "What are you youngins doing in here?"

Elmer's eyes were wide with fright, "Who are you?"

"That's what we want to know, where is the preacher?"

Rufus bolted through the door and caught the calf of the younger intruder and clamped down hard ripping, tearing and delivering a menacing growl. The kid screamed and the tallest of the three took the butt of his shotgun and smacked him unconscious. Blood flowed down the fur of the loyal dog. "What's the matter, kid? A little ole mutt git the best of you?"

Elmer began to cry and Nan ran to comfort him. Maybe Rufus wasn't dead. She certainly hoped not.

The men smelled rotten and were very unsteady on their feet. The elder man looked from Elmer to Nan, "So, kid, how about some of them beans?"

"Okay," said Nan shakily.

"Hurry, boy, we're hungry."

"Nan, who are these men?" asked Elmer.

Elaine Littau

"Nan, huh? Say, Johnson, this is a little girl!"

"Don't say? C'Mere sweetie," said the older one with no front teeth. "Why don't you sit on ole' grandpa's lap?'

They began laughing and grabbing at her. She darted around the cabin, but it was too small. One of them held Elmer while the other two savagely tore at her clothes.

"We hit the mother load, boys. This ain't no little gal. She is full grown."

They yipped in drunken glee as they threw her around the room like a rag doll. Elmer screamed at the top of his lungs. A big fist hit him square in the forehead. He lay lifeless on the floor. Nan squeezed her eyes tight and prayed with all her might that Fred would come and rescue them.

The morning sun broke through the window and cast eerie shadows across the floor. Nan tried to open her eyes, but they were swollen shut from the blows delivered to her head. She was naked and bruised. She tried to get up but the pain seared through her body. She sobbed quietly so as not to awaken the snoring beasts lying in the room. It was too late. The youngest, red-headed one saw her move and headed toward her. "Nanny girl, if you wouldn't fight so hard, 'em fellers would treat ya right kind like." He smiled at her showing tobacco stained teeth. "Come here, sweetheart, let Danny make it all better."

Nan couldn't believe that he would want to ravage her again. "Please God, spare me!" she screamed in her head.

"Kid, stop it! She needs to rest if she is gonna make it to our camp."

Camp? Oh no, not camp! Nan didn't know what to do. *Where was Elmer?* She turned her head and saw him in the same spot he fell last night. *Was he dead?* Nan wished that she were.

The men roused and grabbed some supplies. They refused to let Nan dress. They wrapped a blanket around her and tied her like a sausage. They wouldn't allow her to have her shoes either. "Girl, we don't want you getting' away from us. You belong to us now."

Chapter Twelve

The snow had finally stopped falling on the top of the mountain. Fred had already placed the packs on the mule and horse and was leading them through the hip high snow. He knew the trail, but he also knew the danger of avalanche so he traveled carefully. The stars were beginning to come out when he reached the cabin. The lantern was not burning. Perhaps the kids had already gone to bed. Still, Rufus would have barked a greeting to him. He quietly entered the cabin and was astonished at what he saw. The whole cabin was trashed. Everything he owned was on the floor in heaps. He heard a low moan over by the fireplace. It was Elmer. Rufus was dead. "Elmer? Nan?"

"Nan, where are you?" Fred shouted. "Elmer, what happened?"

He turned the little body toward him and cradled him in his arms. He rose from the floor and lit the lantern. Elmer had a big lump on his forehead and he was as pale as a sheet. Blood was all over the floor and all over Rufus' fur. "Elmer! Wake up!" Fred got a rag and plunged it into the ice-cold bucket of water beside the table and began to mop Elmer's face. Slowly Elmer's eyes opened. "Oh, Fred!"

"Where is Nan?"

"Them three bad men hurt her!"

Fred's blood boiled. What did those trappers want with a little kid like Nan? "Are you sure?"

"No, but they tore her clothes almost off her and hit me so I couldn't help her. They hurt our dog when he tried to help us. Where is Nan? Is Rufus alright?"

Fred's stomach lurched. Those sorry, good-for-nothin' tramps! "Elmer, Nan isn't here and Rufus is dead. You don't look so good. How long ago did this happen?"

Elmer's voice cracked as he spoke, "We were startin to eat some supper when they came. Fred, my head is bustin."

Fred looked at the coals in the hearth and realized that the supper that had been interrupted had been last night.

"Poor kid. Get some rest and we will go find Nan at first light."

Fred fixed Elmer a little watery oatmeal and put him in the big bed. Fred slept little and tried to pray most of the night. As soon as dawn started appearing, Fred had Elmer bundled up and Sonny ready to go. Elmer looked terrible. His lips were as white as the rest of his face. Fred knew that he couldn't take Elmer to find Nan. He had thought about this fact half the night. There was one person that he trusted to take care of this child. His Mother and Dad would have a fit if they every heard tell of it, but it was his only choice. He arrived in Silverton just as the sun was up. He turned the horse up Blair Street to a known house of ill repute. Knocking on the door with Elmer in his arms was as awkward as anticipating the talk with the woman inside. An extremely sleepy woman opened the door with makeup streaked across her unwashed face. The young woman looked years older than her actual years. "Hey, preacher! What are you doin' here? Didn't backslide agin did ya?"

"Betsy, I need your help. Can you watch this little kid for me for a few days? Somebody almost killed him and I need to track him down and take him to the law."

"I ain't no babysitter!"

"I know, but you are the only one that I trust here. Really the only person I know here."

"A few days?'

"Yep"

"Well, maybe…"

"Can you doctor him too? He has a powerful headache too."

"Okay…but."

"Thanks!"

With that he handed over the sleeping Elmer and gently woke him up.

"Elmer, I need you to stay here with Betsy. I'm going to get Nan now. Be good."

"Nan?" Betsy's eyebrows rose dramatically.

"It's his sister. A long story...thanks"

Fred sped through the town and went back to the place where he saw the last tracks the trappers left. Hour after hour he trekked through the deep snow. It was noon when he saw the bunch camped in a clearing beside a creek. He scanned the campsite to see signs of Nan. There she was slumped beside a tree, wrapped in a blanket with no shoes. "Poor kid!" He saw the men squatted beside a small fire. He checked his shotgun and headed into their camp with it cradled in his arms. "Howdy fellers, what are you doing with my kid?"

"Kid? I ain't seen no kid. Have you, Dan?"

"No sir. I ain't seen no kid today!" They erupted in wicked laughter.

"This is my kid!" screamed Fred.

"I don't know who you are tryin to fool old man, but that woman ain't no kid."

"Woman?"

"Yep, and she is just the kind I like. Just take what you want and ya don't even have to pay nor nothin'"

Fred's blue eyes were blue flames ready to ignite a forest fire. "You sorry excuse for a human! Shut your mouth! She is just a little girl! What have you done to her?" Fred didn't wait for an answer, but began to empty his shotgun. One of the men fell dead and one was wounded by stray shot. The kid was approaching camp and saw Fred shooting up the camp. He took aim with his rifle and missed his target. He didn't want to let the girl go back to the Preacher man. "Les, I think I can take him! Throw me your shotgun!"

The wounded man cursed his companion and yelled at Fred, "Get your woman out of here and leave us be! She ain't worth dyin' fer."

"Speak fer yourself! I want to keep her!"

"Shut your mouth, Dan! She ain't worth it! Git yourself over here and help me before he kills us too!"

The two thugs scampered into the brush out of sight.

When Fred put his hand out to help Nan to her feet, she screamed. Fred firmly declared, "Nan, its me, Fred!"

"Go away! I never want to see you again. I just want to die!"

"I'm here to take you home."

"Home?"

"To the cabin."

"Fred?"

"Come on little one, let me get you home. Then I will go get Elmer."

"Elmer? Is he…?"

"He is being taken care of."

"Can we get Elmer first?"

"Okay…" Fred ran that thought through and decided that perhaps Betsy could help Nan. It was obvious to Fred that she had been ill-used. He would have to make sure that Betsy treated her delicately because of her innocence.

Carefully he placed her on his horse and wrapped her with his blanket. He placed his poncho over it and wrapped her feet with rags so the frostbite could be kept to a minimum. He led Sonny slowly down the slope. He knew that she needed help, yet he dreaded bringing her into town for prying eyes to see. He saw to it that they arrived in Silverton at nightfall.

Betsy opened the door at his knock. "Fred?"

"Yes. I'm back with the boy's sister. Can you help me?"

"What is it this time?"

"Some filthy scum got a hold of her and…you know. She is just a kid and they treated her bad. She needs doctoring from a woman."

"You have this crazy notion that I am a doctor or somthin.' Where did you git that idea?"

"You know more about stuff than I do. Please help."

After taking Nan into her room and cleaning her wounds, Betsy emerged into the parlor. "Fred, she is hurt bad. It may take days for her to be her old self, so wait a week or two before you lie with her again."

"What! Are you crazy? I wouldn't touch a child!"

"She is no child, hun! She is all of fifteen or sixteen!"

"That can't be! She has been living with me for months! It isn't proper for her to live with me in the middle of nowhere!"

"Well, it ain't proper what them fellers did to her either! I can guarantee that she is with child after all the things that happened."

"With child! Oh no!"

"Are you trying to tell me that she has lived with you for months and you didn't know she was a woman and you never lay with her?"

"Of course I never touched her!"

"Nobody will believe that now. You might as well leave her here with me to be a working girl. She is ruined for ordinary life!"

Fred's head was spinning. Nan had already been through so much even before coming to the mountains. Now this? What could he do? He would have to spare her embarrassment. How could he protect her? He would marry her. No one would have to know what had happened to her. How could this have happened? Would she know that she needed to marry him for his protection?

Just then Nan entered the room. She looked so tired and weak. Betsy had given her a plain calico dress and moccasins.

"How old are you, Nan?"

"I will be sixteen next month." She began to weep.

"Nan, I know what happened to you. I know that you are probably expecting a baby now.

Nan's eyes grew wide, "A baby?"

"I know that so called decent people won't understand or believe what happened to you because you have been on the mountain with me for all these months."

"What…?"

"Please don't cry! It isn't your fault."

"I'm not a bad girl! Am I a bad girl now, after….this?"

"I want you to marry me today…"

"Marry you? I couldn't do that to you!"

"So everyone will think that your child, if one comes along after your ordeal, is mine. He won't have to face the world with shame."

"Shame? I brought shame?…on you…a baby? What?"

"Marry me, Nan. For your sake and…the baby."

"I don't know…I'm so tired…"

"Nan, I want to take care of you. I won't touch you in any improper way. You will have the chance to decide if you love me later. You need protection now and so will your child."

Elmer was standing in the doorway, "Nan, do you have a child?"

"Elmer! I thought you were a goner! Are you all right? You are alive? I have been so afraid for you." Elmer's forehead was wrapped in a clean cloth and his face was still too pale.

"Elmer, Fred wants me to marry him."

"Will that make us a real family, Nan?"

"Fred?"

"Yes, Elmer, we will be a real family!"

"Now, ain't that sweet." Exclaimed the hostess of the house. Betsy couldn't believe her ears that any man would do such a thing. "Fred, why didn't ya ask me to marry you when you spent so much time paying for me way back when?"

Nan looked at Fred wince at the remark. "Betsy, I was a very sick man back then. I am sorry for the way I treated you."

Fred turned to see the look of disappointment shade Nan's face. "Nan lets go see the Justice of the Peace and then head home."

"I don't know."

"Do it, Nan, this man isn't all bad. Give him a chance. Give your baby a chance." Betsy wiped tears away from her rough face.

The Justice of the Peace looked at the bedraggled assortment of humanity standing at his door. First, the young man with a determined look on his face, then a very young girl whose face was beaten and bleeding, and of course, the small boy who had a bandage around his head. He knew there had to be a story in all this, but he wasn't sure he wanted to deal with whatever it was. "State your business," Declared the Justice of the Peace.

"We are here to be married, sir," answered the young man.

"You don't say?" The older man looked intently at the young girl and saw nothing of the excitement that a bride would have. "Girl, do you want to be married?"

Nan just shrugged. She barely knew what was happening to her. She was so tired and couldn't think straight.

"Okay, that will be two bits."

Fred fished the money from his shirt pocket and handed it to the man.

"I'll make this plain and simple. I don't see any use in hearts and flowers for the two of you by the way things look from this perspective...Girl, do you take this man for a husband?"

"Yes," Nan's voice croaked. She knew that it was her only hope for a normal life.

"Mister, do you take this...her for your wife?"

"Yes." Tears threatened his eyes. Fred knew that he didn't love this girl other than the love for a sister, but he knew that he could never really love anyone but Claire for the rest of his life. As bad as it was, he was grateful for the plain ceremony. He could never bear going through all the poetic words that aptly described his love for his dead wife. He would help Nan get through this if it killed him."

"Well then, you're married. Good day."

Fred put Nan and Elmer on Sonny and lead him through the busy town and toward the vast wilderness of the mountains.

Elaine Littau

They would all be able to heal at the cabin. He would take care of them. He would get them through this. The thought pounded his brain. "Get through this…get through this."

Nan just about fell off the horse and Fred caught her just in time. "It isn't much farther, Nan, hang on."

He noticed tears dripping from her chin. He couldn't see her eyes because of the swelling from the beating. *That judge probably thought that I did that to her. When is enough, enough? Lord, You have got to improve the state of her life!* As they plodded along, Fred prayed to his God. A cold chill ran down his back as he remembered that he had killed one of the trappers. He had never killed anyone before. He wasn't sorry for what he had done. Would God answer any of his prayers now? Just then the cabin came into site. He carried first Nan and then Elmer into the cabin. He then put Sonny in the barn, fed and watered him, and made his way to the house. There had not been nearly as much snow in this spot as there was up the mountain. When he entered the cabin, Nan was sitting on the end of the bed all bent over. Her posture was that of an elderly woman. Elmer was asleep in the trundle bed. Nan had tucked him in and rubbed camphor on his brow. The odor stung Fred's eyes. Nan seemed to be unaware of Fred's presence. Fred came to Nan and put his hand on hers. "Nan, get in bed with Elmer and I'll tuck you in."

She bent her head back and looked at him through the slits in her eyes. She was so grateful to be back and safe with Fred. Nodding, she climbed into the unoccupied side of the bed. He tucked the quilts up to her chin and got out several woolen blankets and spread them over the pair in the bed. He walked up to the fireplace and began starting a fire in the cold hearth. As he was patiently tending the tiny flame and feeding the kindling to the fire, the Lord gave him a revelation of his future with Nan. He was assured that what had begun in tragedy would turn into something warm and beautiful. It would take a lot of time to start a flame of love, but God was the God of creation. He spoke the world into existence and He could bring love into a cold heart. Fred felt that God was pleased with him for marrying Nan. He was going to be with them in all of these troubles. Fred added a stack of wood to the flames and soon had a roaring fire. It was as if God were telling him that the love they would eventually share would be strong and good like this fire had turned out to be. He was reminded of the Scripture, "I will return to you the years that the locusts have eaten." Could that really happen in his life? What if there was a child on the way? "My grace is sufficient for you." He turned and looked at the young battered girl sleeping in the bed and wondered.

Chapter Thirteen

Mary was surprised that the people of the town responded in kindness when interest was shown to them. She had always been a social outcast because she never had the nerve to risk being rejected by other people. Well, she was thirty-two years old now and she had decided to do or die. Her first attempts at making friends were quite shaky and awkward, but there was amazing progress. She had walked into the dry goods store and asked to see the stationary. When Sarah, the proprietress, raised her eyebrows at the request, Mary proceeded to recite the made up story of writing to her darling stepchildren and how she did hope and pray that they were enjoying their visit with the relatives in Boston. Upon completing the fabrication, Mary lowered her voice as if asking a question in grave confidence to Sarah Brown, "Can you tell me if the large church in the center of town is open socially to newcomers?"

"Mrs. Dewey, of course!"

"I don't know if you understand my meaning, Mrs. Brown, but I am tired of the seclusion of the farm and wish to make myself available to any committees, clubs, or other appropriate organized groups that the church sponsors." Mrs. Dewy's throat was beginning to become very dry and parched. The words had a scratchy sound to them and Mary was hoping that her case of nerves was not as apparent to Mrs. Brown.

"Oh, I see. Yes, they are always in need of members to the ladies missionary society and of course the church festivities group always needs fresh members to dream up fundraisers for the community. If you make yourself known to Prudence Malone, the president of the women's society of the church, she will put you on so many committees that your head will spin. Your husband, if he is like mine, will make you limit the functions you attend because you will become quite busy, that is, if Mrs. Malone takes a liking to you."

"Would it be possible for you to arrange an introduction to Mrs. Malone for me?"

"I hardly know you!" Mrs. Brown looked quite concerned that such a request would come from a virtual stranger.

Mary almost lost her nerve. If this were to work she would have to give it her best effort. Clearing her throat, Mary forced courage and a bit of dignity into her voice. "Mrs. Brown, the only reason that we are not better acquainted is because I have had enormous responsibility tending to two unfortunate orphans. Until recently I have not had so much as a moment to look up from the work and care of nurturing those precious children. My heart is fairly broken now that they are on this extended visit. The eldest cousin of Nan and Elmer has asked me to consider letting the great aunt adopt them and raise them close to all their kin. As you might imagine, I am at a loss as to what to do with the void in my life. Mr. Dewey is staying with his dying mother and I just wish to make myself useful to whomever might benefit from my services."

"Dear me! Yes, I suppose I might be able to arrange a meeting between you and Mrs. Malone. You will take tea with us when it can be arranged at my home. I will send word to you on the day and time. You do know where my house is?"

"Of course," Mary lied. "Thank you for your assistance in this matter." Mary managed a friendly smile as she made her purchase of chicken feed. She would have to go to the mercantile across the street for yard goods so that Mrs. Brown wouldn't know that the dress she wore for tea was stitched especially for the occasion. *Occasion? Yes, of course it was an occasion.* She felt like a debutante at a coming out party. Maybe this would be the key to acceptance that she had longed for all her life.

Mary worked long into the night on the dress. She toiled over every stitch trying to make it perfect. One good quality Mary had was determination, and she was determined to make a good impression. The chicken feed dress would have to wait until next week. Morning blazed into her room and she hopped out of bed chiding herself for sleeping so late. She hurried through the chores, promising herself that she would do a much better job the next time.

She had to add some culture to her vocabulary. Daily she had studied the one book that had escaped the shipment to Boston. It was a rare novel that had belonged to Nancy. Mary had at first thought that the language was quite uppity, but then realized that people in social circles probably spoke like that. How would she learn to speak like this? She decided to just use a few of the phrases that struck her as the most cultured. She noticed that people said "children" instead of "kids" or "youngins" and spoke in a quiet way. She looked through the book to see if any references were made to tea-time. Luckily, the mistress of the house had a good many callers and prepared tea quite regularly. The book spoke of the little cakes eaten with the pinky finger extended. Mary got the last piece of cornbread from the pan. It was cold and hard but edible even if it was left over from the night before. She also read about the large linen napkins that were to be draped over the lap.

"Goodness sakes, it is plum stupid to put the napkin there, a whole lot of food could end up down the front of your dress that way. I wish they put the napkin into the neck of their dress like normal folk!" So with a dry dishcloth and her cold cornbread and hot coffee, Mary practiced the art of being a lady taking tea with the social elite. After her hours of practice she began the chore of cleaning up the dishes. As she dried the few things that she had washed, she noticed her hands. My, but they were red and callused. She remembered that her mother had rubbed horse medicine over her hands and elbows to soften them up. Being a lady was such a bother, but Mrs. Malone might not know the hard work a lone woman had to do on a farm. When she got the message that she was to come to Mrs. Brown's house, she would ask the messenger where the house was located and then have to take a bath. That would be a lot of work too. Was it all worth it? Mary heard the clock on the mantle chime and realized that she was quite behind on her evening chores. She would do without supper tonight. She was too anxious to eat anyway.

After the meeting with Mrs. Malone, Mary kept a busy pace in the social circles of the large church in the center of town. She became a regular at the Monday morning quilting circle and the Tuesday afternoon bridge club. Never mind that she had to rise earlier and go to bed later to keep up the break-neck pace. She had new friends and acquaintances. If there was to be an event, Mary was called upon to participate in it. It didn't seem to bother her that she was never called upon to chair any particular event. Goodness knows that she really didn't know much about such matters, but she did have a stubborn will and desire to learn all the things that she put her efforts into. It was after one of the mornings of quilting that she walked into the farmhouse to discover Mr. Dewey sitting at the kitchen table drinking a cup of lukewarm coffee. "Where have you been this fine morning, Mrs. Dewey?"

Mary didn't like the smirk that lurked in the corner or his mouth. "Why, I have been at the church quilting bee, Mr. Dewey. How is your Mother?"

"She has passed away, my dearest Mary." He was studying the appearance of Mary and couldn't quite put a finger on the difference in her looks. "Did you take those two kids to town with you or what?"

"I sent them to Boston to live with their great aunt. She wrote and was quite firm about their living with her. She did say that the place is ours if we care to keep it seeing that we took care of them all these months." The lie was so familiar to Mary by now that it seemed to be the truth to her.

Sam studied her face and decided that she was speaking the truth. He wasn't at all sure that he liked the idea of a woman making a decision like this without him, but it had to be easier

Elaine Littau

to get by with two less mouths to feed. Of course they did earn their keep, at least Nan did. What was Mary up to? She was all gussied up for something. "Have you made a good number of friends since I have been gone, dear wife?"

Mary didn't like the tone that Sam was using. She would have to be very careful about how she answered him. "Not so many as you might think. I have managed to make a few acquaintances that may be beneficial to us. It may be to our advantage to have people speak well of us...say, if we were ever to want to get a loan for improvements or start a small enterprise."

At that Sam gave a small chuckle. "Well said, good woman. You know how to butter your bread on both sides, now don't you?"

"So, you are home for good now, or is there other business with your family's estate that you have to finish up?"

"Got it all sewed up day before yesterday. I'm here to stay. Come to me, Mary. I might get the idea that you aren't glad to see me."

"Well Sam, you have been gone so long, I thought that you might have just decided to stay away. You didn't write or try to get word to me. You haven't been home for months."

"Get over here!"

Mary gingerly walked over to Sam. She was almost afraid to look him in the eye. She didn't know exactly what kind of mood he was in. Things certainly were a lot less complicated when he was gone.

As Mary came across the room, Sam was struck with the subtle changes in her. Maybe he would wait a while before taking action, if any, on the news that she gave him today. She had a softer, more feminine look about her. He noticed that her eyes were a deep shade of blue, like the calico dress she wore. Her sunbonnet had slipped to expose her brown hair. It was different. It looked good and she smelled like vanilla. "Mary, I am very hungry and couldn't find anything in the makings. I want dinner now."

Mary thought better than to answer him with a strong retort. Actually, he had never been this kind to her. "How about some sourdough biscuits and gravy? I'll fix a proper supper by sundown."

"Sounds good to me." Sam was amazed that she took his order so casually. Maybe having a wife at home to take care of him was better than memory served.

Mary woke up before daybreak to the sound of Sam's snoring. She was strangely glad to have him back and yes, even in her bed. There was a comfort in having a man around that defies description. He had held her close just a moment after the act of marriage. There was almost tenderness in it. Mary could only hope that things wouldn't deteriorate like they had before he left to see about his mother. He had the ability to be extremely cruel. He had made a comment about the fact that she was an old maid when he "rescued" her from spinsterhood. She had answered him back angrily and told him that she had another offer of marriage a few years back. When Sam found out that her intended had run off with her younger cousin who was established better financially, he laughed at her and mocked her because she obviously was still nursing a broken heart. Mary was so angry that she slapped his face. He then punched her so hard that she lost her breath. That was the first time he took a hand to her. He had started calling her names and making her feel degraded. Somehow, since his return she was in his good graces. She was going to have to watch her step and be sure to keep from upsetting him. She smiled when she thought of the conversation they had when he first got home and how she had matched wits with him. He seemed to like that. She would try to be interesting to him. Maybe she would be fortunate enough to have a child. No one would ever call her a spinster again. She turned toward Sam and fell back to sleep watching him as he snored. In two short hours Mary awoke for the day. She studied her face in the glass as

Elaine Littau

she brushed her long brown hair. There were plenty of women who were much better looking than she was, but there were many more that were not. She decided that she fit somewhere in the middle. The excitement of Sam's being home again had brought some color into her cheeks and the daily administration of cow medicine and salve to her hands and face had softened the ruddy completion. She had not realized that taking pains on her appearance gave her a more pleasing countenance and that practicing her manners, choice of words, and voice inflection were making a notable difference in her overall feminine appeal.

She donned the same new blue calico print dress that she wore upon Sam's homecoming. She usually wore one of her old dresses when she was at home, but somehow she felt more confident in her new dress. Her eyes sparkled just a little as she started frying eggs and sausage in the pan. She placed some biscuits into the oven just as Sam made his way to the table and pulled his chair out to sit down. She brought him a cup and poured the fragrant coffee into it. She put the sugar bowl on the table with his teaspoon. "Sam, I remember that you like a little sugar in your coffee and no cream. Is that still to your liking?"

Sam paused his spoon in mid flight to the sugar bowl and wondered just who this woman was that was living in his house. She certainly didn't sound like the Mary Dewey that he had left some seven months ago. The old Mary put a meal on as if she were slopping hogs or something. "Yep, that'll do." He had to be careful or she would get the upper hand on him. A smile slipped to his lips before he could squelch it. *Man, it was good to be married again.* He had forgotten how much enjoyment a man could acquire in the arms of a wife. He mustn't let it go to his head or she would be able to wrap him around her little finger. One thing about Mary, she was a healthy woman with no recollection of a wonderful dead husband. She ought to be able to give him the son that he wanted. The "namesake" was necessary for him to obtain his inheritance from his father. Clarence Dewey had specifically stated in his will that not one penny would be left to Sam until a son was born to him and named Clarence Samuel Dewey III. It didn't hurt that the tide had turned and she appeared to be more agreeable and even a sight better to look at than she had been. He would keep her in line though. A well-landed punch could do the trick. He would have to not hit her in the stomach until after the boy child had been born and now that she was into the society...well, there were other ways to keep control of a sassy wife.

Mary saw the smile cross his face and blushed to think of what probably put it there. She smiled too. She was very glad that she still had all of her teeth and could smile a full, happy smile. *"It is true, you do get a lot more flies with honey that with vinegar! We'll see how far this 'killing with kindness' will take me."* Mary thought as she put the eggs and sausage onto their plates. This was a sight better than the complaining and grunting mornings of the past. Maybe Sam was like the townspeople. The smile reappeared. *People are such fools, you don't even have to mean it, just act like you like them and they fall for it every time!* The memory of the last beating Sam gave her was enough to keep this playacting going indefinitely. Maybe she could learn to love him. She had sworn never to love another man again after Lester had run off with Cousin Mildred, but she deserved happiness if she could latch onto some. She smelled the biscuits baking and knew that it was time to get them out before they were too brown or burned altogether for goodness sake! They were perfect. What luck! Sam would never believe this. After the satisfying breakfast, Sam made his way to the barn and began the work of a farmer while Mary cleaned the kitchen and was so thankful to only have to do "woman's work." Today was washday, so she changed into her oldest dress and began heating the wash water the old wood stove. She dug through Sam's bedroll and found a wad of filthy clothes and long-handle underwear. She rifled through the pockets of his pants and got out his

Elaine Littau

pocketknife and various other odds and ends that men always carried. His pocket watch was in the watch pocket. She opened it and saw the image of his mother. Maybe one day he would care enough of her to put her photograph in his watch. That was a lost cause. He loved his mother to a fault. Mary had never been privileged enough to meet the "Sainted Mother" of Sam Dewey. *Just take one step at a time, Mary. This is hard enough for now.*

Chapter Fourteen

Nan grew stronger with every passing day. Her eyes had only traces of black in the inside corners, and the swelling was all but gone. Fred watched her with concern across his brow. *How could one so young endure so much physical abuse in her short life?* He was glad that he had married her so he could protect her, and for that matter, Elmer too. Elmer was suffering more since the attack. The headaches were cruel and lingering. Elmer had suffered four days solid before he had a short time of relief. Nan tended to him with camphor and cool wet rags. Fred knew that he had to get Elmer off the mountain to see a doctor before long, but he was afraid that his and Nan's health was too fragile for the trip. He had made up his mind to take them to Denver to see a top-notch doctor as soon as they could stand it if the doctor at Trinidad didn't have any answers for him. Silent tears traced the smooth tanned cheeks as he lay in the dark making the plans to go. Nan cried out in her sleep and awakened him. She gave muffled cries throughout the days since he had found her and brought her home. She slept a lot; it was as if she were avoiding being awake at all. Of course the poor kid was worn out because of the lack of sleep and taking care of Elmer. Fred had not let her do any work around the place until she healed up. Maybe he had been wrong not to let her keep busy, but he was afraid that the strain might just kill her. She spoke in quiet, reassuring tones to Elmer, but no words for Fred. She was jumpy all the time. If an owl or coyote called, she was on edge. What was he going to do to help her? Finally, just before daybreak, he knew what he would have to do. She felt defenseless. He had let her down by not being there when she needed him. He would give her the means to defend herself. He climbed out of bed and put his woolen pants over his long johns and donned his red wool shirt and suspenders.

"Nan, wake up. We have a big day today!"

Nan slowly opened her eyes and looked at Fred with dead eyes. "Elmer needs more sleep; he fretted all night last night. I think this one must be a real bad one."

"That's alright, Nan, we can let Elmer sleep. I need to talk to you."

Nan avoided Fred's eyes. The blue orbs seemed to see all the way to her soul. Her soul felt dirty and bruised and unfit to be examined. "Is everything alright?"

"No, Nan. Everything isn't alright." If she had looked up at him she would have seen the glint of a tear on his face. "I know how you are feeling."

"How could you know how I am feeling? I don't know how I am feeling. I feel dead inside. I feel abandoned by…God… man…you…my mama…papa…" She covered her face with her hands and she sobbed uncontrollably.

Fred didn't want to scare her so he didn't know whether to put his hand on her shoulder or not. He wanted to comfort her. He decided to put as much comfort in his words as he could muster, "Nan, I failed you and Elmer. I wasn't here. You know why I left, but I shouldn't have left you defenseless. I intend to see that you will never be in that condition again. I am going to teach you how to defend yourself."

Nan stopped crying and took a long deep breath. Sobs were still wracking her small frame. She looked up at him and saw the determined look in his eyes and also the traces the tears had made on his cheeks. She knew that he meant what he said. "What do you have in mind?"

"I was going to teach both you and Elmer how to shoot this shotgun, but I don't think Elmer is really strong enough. I will have to wait to teach him until he is feeling better. I have been watching you and I know that you are scared to death of those two men who are still out there."

Nan began to cry and twisted her handkerchief in her hands. Just the mention of those men made her blood run cold.

"I'm sorry, but we both know what you have been thinking. You are afraid that what happened could happen again or that they might kill you and Elmer next time. I intend for you to be able to defend yourself."

Nan nodded, "Yes, Fred, I want to learn. I will try my best."

"I have a rifle, but I think the shotgun would serve you best. It has a kick to it, but it also has two shots. That way you won't have to reload if you miss or if both of them come at you."

Nan swallowed hard. Having her fears put out in the open with words was hard to take.

"First, I am going to show you how to hold the gun from where I stand. Then, I am going to have to stand close to you a bit to make sure you see how to hold the gun. I don't want to scare you by being too close, but I promise I won't hurt you."

He spoke to her so softly that she had to listen carefully to hear every word. Even though she knew that Fred would never harm her, it was hard to be near him. He worked carefully to make her feel at ease. She was like a wild animal that was out of its natural surroundings. He wanted her to feel comfortable around him and to know that he had no intentions of hurting her. She was shaking as he said, "Put the butt of the shotgun to your shoulder like so, and stand with your legs slightly apart. You want to anchor yourself so that when the shot goes off, it won't knock you to the ground. It has a kick to it, see. Hold it tight. Look down the barrel and line up the site with the target. Try to center it on the target, but don't worry if it isn't just right. It is a shotgun and will hit anything you aim at. I want you to try it and see what it feels like. Now squeeze the trigger easy like. I know you are still hurt and such, but this lesson can't wait."

Elaine Littau

The gun was heavier than Nan thought it would be. The barrel seemed very long and awkward. She brought it up to her shoulder and tried to steady it.

"Take a deep breath, Nan, and pull the trigger."

She sucked in some air and closed her eyes as she pulled the trigger. *Bam*. Down she went. She jumped up quickly and dusted the snow off. "Sorry."

"Good first try. Do it again. Brace yourself. Plant your feet. Now."

The second shot went off and Nan was still standing. Her shoulder hurt like fire, but she was still on her feet.

"Let me show you how to load this thing."

Nan watched carefully and shot again and again until she was reasonably sure that she could hit the broad side of a barn if need be.

As they were walking back to the cabin, she realized that the trembling inside her had stopped. She knew that she could take care of Elmer and herself. Somehow she began to feel peaceful…Just a little.

"I'm much obliged to you for teaching me this."

"Do you think you can shoot, that is, if you need to?"

"I can do anything if need be."

Fred was glad to hear the confidence coming into her voice, "I bet you could! My dad was right. You and Elmer are good little soldiers."

Nan didn't understand why, but that comment made her feel both proud and hurt at the same time. She was glad that he thought that she was brave, but he still thought she was a child. Why did that bother her? She didn't care if she ever saw another man again. Well, Fred was different. He was like a brother to her. No, he was actually her husband. Her husband! Yes, he was her husband, but he was her husband because he wanted to protect her like a brother would. Yes, he was more of a brother and that was fine. He acted like a brother and spoke like a brother. She was glad that he was there to protect them…most of the time.

As soon as the words came out of his mouth, it felt strange to him. *"…Little soldiers?"* His mind was turning. *Now she was brave, but she wasn't a kid and she deserved to be respected as an adult.* He would remember to speak to her as an equal from now on. She was one of the most grown up people in his life. She didn't pout or get selfish no matter what had happened to her. *She did have guts, that is for sure. What a quick study! She had that gun down in no time. What a relief. He had no doubt that she could defend herself and Elmer. Elmer…he needed to speak with her about Elmer before they got to the cabin.* "Nan, I want to ask you something about Elmer."

Nan's eyebrows raised in interest. "Yes?"

"How long have these headaches been going on?"

"He has had them ever since he was three, so I guess, two and a half years. We never took him to a doctor. Mama was too sick to take him and Mr. and Mrs. Dewey never did either."

"I want to take him to see a doctor." He saw her start to shudder, "You must come too."

"…But what about Mr. and Mrs. Dewey? If they happened to see us, what would happen?"

"Wait a minute, Nan, you are my wife and they can't take you away from me even if they did find you."

Nan's eyes grew wide. She had never thought of that.

"I am glad that I married you, even if it just keeps you away from those monsters."

"What about Elmer? Can they take him?"

"Did they adopt him?"

"No."

"Then, I think you have more right to raise him than they do."

Nan smiled for the first time since Fred brought her back to the cabin. "Thank goodness we are safe! Thank you!"

She started to give him a hug, but couldn't bring herself to do it. She stuck out her hand and gave his big hand a firm handshake.

Elaine Littau

Fred was amused in spite of himself. Somehow this firm handshake from his girl bride felt so much more comforting to him than all the nights spent in the house of ill repute in Silverton. They were going to be good friends and that was all right with him. There were many times when he needed a good friend.

The next few weeks Fred made preparations for a meager Christmas celebration for his little family. He cut a tree down and sawed it into rough boards. He spent many hours using a hand planer to smooth them into smooth, clean boards. He fashioned a beautiful clothes cupboard from it and oiled it to preserve it and enhance the grain of the pine. He knew that Nan would find it pretty. He worked tirelessly next to the fireplace after Elmer had gone to bed whittling little birds and forest creatures for Elmer's Christmas present. Nan sat next to him attempting to crochet a long wool scarf for Elmer. It appeared to take her an awfully long time to work on one scarf. Nan had devised a plan to work on two scarves at the same time. She made them of the same color wool and care-fully slipped the needle from one in progress to the other each evening. They were finished practically at the same time. They sat in silence for the most part as they worked each evening, but the conversations they did share were quiet and meaning-ful. Nan told Fred all the things she remembered about her Mama and Papa and the life they lived together in her memory of the "golden days." Fred identified with her on that because he felt much the same way about his childhood and previous marriage and fatherhood. As she spoke, the tenderness on her face was so touching. She was lovely to look upon. Her dark hair brushed her shoulders now and she tied it back with a rag when she was doing chores. She let it hang loose while they spent their evenings together. She was still thin and small and he worried about her getting enough rest. Many times before

Christmas Elmer cried for hours as he suffered. Nan and Fred took turns tending to him as best as they could.

Christmas Day dawned and Fred brought a sapling into the cabin. He had decorated it with some cotton from the storage shed. It looked like fresh fallen snow. He could not bring himself to put Joy and Claire's decorations on the tree. It still seemed too soon. The house was fragrant from the quail Fred snared earlier. Nan was becoming a good cook. Fred brought a bundle to Elmer. It was a beaver pelt expertly tanned and tied together with a strip of leather. It was holding precious contents.

"Elmer this is for you. You may sell the pelt or trade it for something you want, but untie the leather and you will see another gift from me to you."

Elmer's eyes shone as he felt the softness of the pelt and untied it. He unfolded the skin and found the most stunning carvings he had ever seen. There were two cardinals and a little squirrel. They looked as if they could jump to life at any time.

"Oh Fred! I love 'em! Thank you!" Elmer shyly brought a little object to Fred. "I didn't have anything to wrap this in, but I looked until I found something that made me think of you. Elmer opened his little hand and presented to Fred a beautiful gray quartz stone. He opened his other hand and handed Nan a matching one that was pink quartz.

"Beautiful! Magnificent! Wonderful! Precious!" were the exclamations from the two recipients.

Nan was surprised when Fred told her to close her eyes while he brought in the present that he had for her. "Open your eyes, Nan."

Nan clapped her hand over her mouth. She had never seen anything so beautiful. "It is lovely!"

Fred grinned. How did he know that was what she would say? "It is to put our clothes in. See?"

"Now it is your turn!" She had wrapped the gifts for Elmer and Fred in some of their old shirts that she had mended.

Fred and Elmer unfolded the shirts and the woolen scarves fell to the floor. "Wow, a mended shirt and a new scarf! That great! Isn't that right Pard?"

"Nan, you are such a good sister! Thank you!"

"I would say that this Christmas morning has been a wonderful start to a great day. Let's read the Christmas story from the Bible after we get the food on the table, and we can enjoy the rest of the day.

Fred read the passage from the book of Luke, the second chapter. It was truly beautiful. He had read the first chapter to them before they retired for the night yesterday. Nan pondered the message that this story was telling. Could it really be that a living God sent His Son to live as a man? Fred had told them that the reason for Jesus' coming was to show us the way to God and to show us the love of God. She had always thought of God as a God of judgment and punishment. Fred attempted to show as well as tell them of a God that loved more than a body could understand. Fred was like God in that way. He didn't have to be good to them but he was.

The dinner was tasty and Fred and Elmer ate their fill, but Nan wasn't hungry and picked at her food. The rest of the day was peaceful and sweet. They cared for the animals and watched the snow as it fell softly around the cozy cabin.

Chapter Fifteen

"Everything is packed, Fred." Nan said. All that needed doing was to get Elmer on the horse and they would be ready to go down the mountain to Trinidad where Martha and Nate lived. Fred carried Elmer to Sonny and spoke to Nan, "Get on first, Nan, and I will hand him up to you."

"Won't that be too heavy a load for him to carry so far?"

"You weigh almost nothing. It won't hurt for you to ride," smiled Fred.

Nan scurried to the horse and climbed upon him and reached out her arms for Elmer. He had felt pretty well for two days in a row and Fred had judged him able to travel. Elmer smiled at Nan and looked so happy. "It will be so good to see Nate and Martha. I think of them all the time."

"I do too, Elmer. They were so kind to us." A small frown clouded Nan's face. She couldn't help but wonder what they would think of her becoming their daughter-in-law. How would they take the news? Would Fred tell them?

Fred saw the concern on her face and guessed that she was nervous to be back in civilization. "Nan, it's all right. The Deweys can't hurt you anymore. We already talked about that."

"I know."

"What's the matter then?"

"Your folks have been so good to me. I hate for them to change their minds."

"Why would they change their minds?"

"I'm not exactly *daughter-in-law* material you know."

"They trust me and my judgment, Nan. Don't worry."

He was thinking the same thing. They would be ready to horsewhip him if they thought that he had taken advantage of a young girl in his care. How would he tell them? He knew he could never tell them what had happened to her. Even though they were good Christian people, they would probably think the same way most people thought of girls who had been treated in such a way. Public opinion leaned toward the absurd thought that such a girl was from that point on dirty and unfit to marry. As he looked at the young innocent face questioning him, he determined that no one would ever know how she had been treated by the savage men or about the reasoning behind the unexpected marriage. They started moving on the trail down the mountain. His thoughts were clear and hurried. He would speak to Nan when Elmer slept. He would tell her that they would pretend to share a bed at his parents' house. He would lie down for a minute and mess up his side of the bed, but sleep the night away on the floor. Could she pretend to love him and smile at him the way a new wife would? He would stress to her that her future and the future of her child, if there was a child on the way, would depend on her acting abilities. Could he look at her the same way he looked at Claire? His Ma and Pa wouldn't expect him to love Nan in the same way. He could tell them that he was very fond of Nan and that marriage was the only solution for her safety. They would protest that love was the key ingredient to a good marriage, but he would say that he had already experienced the love of his life and that fondness was better than loneliness.

Fondness, yes he was very fond of Nan. She was a unique young woman. He noticed that since the attack, she neither felt sorry for herself, nor quit taking care of Elmer. If anything, she had become more nurturing toward both Elmer and Fred. She was grateful that Fred had married her and that he cared about Elmer and her. She had the buffalo robe tucked around her and Elmer and a heavy-hooded robe over her that covered most of her face. He looked in her direction and missed seeing her eyes. As he trudged along in the deep snow, visions of the young girl and her brother crept into his mind. He thought of one of the fishing days of the autumn and how her black hair had been so short. It brushed her chin and gave her the look of a mischievous boy. Only...the eyes...yes, her eyes were lively and sparkling. He guessed that the fondness began at that moment. He had thought that she was a kid, but he felt a closeness to her begin at that instant. "The twinkling of an eye," a mere split second and he felt a kinship grow between them. He heard tell of many a man who had a wife that he could barely tolerate. It wasn't so bad to have a wife that you liked as a friend. In fact, that might be the best kind of wife to have, that is, since Claire was gone.

Nan sat quietly as the trail wound down the mountain. Fred was so unusually still that she became uneasy. He was probably dreading the thought of introducing her to his parents as his new wife. She hated to think of him regretting the decision that he had made. He had gone from being a bachelor with no one to take care of to being responsible for two, no three, other people. Yes, she was going to have a baby. The thought of it scared her. She hoped that the little one would not remind her of any of the trappers. She was determined not to look for a resemblance. After all, it was not the little baby's fault that he was on his way. She would have to ask Martha many questions about caring for a baby. She wished that she could spend a good many days with Martha, but she knew that the most important thing for now was taking care of Elmer. She didn't know how to tell Fred about the baby. She should, after all, that is the reason that he had married her. Fred was such a good man. He deserved better than her, but it was his decision and she was glad that in that decision came her and her brother's freedom from the Deweys. She would be sure that he never would regret the kindness that he had shown them. She would be obedient and work hard and make him proud of her somehow.

"Nan, since Elmer is asleep, we need to talk about this visit with my family."

"Yes, Fred."

"How good of an actress are you?"

"Actress?"

"Nan, I need you pretend a little when we get to Ma and Pa's house. You will need to look at me sorta like I'm the man you love. We will share a room, but I will sleep on the floor so that they will think that we are really husband and wife."

"I see...Fred, I do love you a little."

Fred blinked back tears of disbelief, "You do?"

"You have treated me better than anyone since my ma and pa died. You have given your life up for me and my brother!"

"I love you a little too, Nan. You and Elmer have given me a new purpose in life. Before you came along, I thought that there was nothing for me in this life. I was ready to just curl up and die." Fred could hardly believe that he was telling her these things. Well, why shouldn't he, she was his wife and when he married her it was forever. He decided that it wouldn't be too hard to look at her with affection. After all, he really did love her...a little.

"Fred, I have something that I need to tell you. I have to tell you before I lose my nerve. I am expecting a baby! I am scared to death and don't know anything about it except that having babies and losing them is what killed my ma."

"Oh Nan! Are you feeling all right? Will you be able to...I don't know...love him? And take care of him?"

"The baby is innocent. I will love him and take care of him as best I can. I do need to ask your ma some questions about everything. Can you let them know what happened to me? I just can't talk about it."

"I will tell Ma and Pa that we are having a baby. I will tell no one about the terrible things that you went through. People usually don't forget or let you forget about things like that, and I want you to be able to put this all behind you. From this point on, I am the father of that baby. I will think of him as mine for the rest of my life. The child need never know anything different. I don't want my child to be called names and taunted all of his life. You are my wife and what happens to you happens to me. You will never have to talk or hear about that attack again. If you ever need to talk about it, you can talk to me and we will get through this."

"What are you going to say to your folks about us getting married?"

"I'm going to tell them that when I found out how old you were, I decided that it was not proper for you to live with me without being married to me and that I had grown so fond of you and Elmer that I could not bear the thought of your leaving me on the mountain alone."

"Will they believe that?"

"They should. It is the truth."

Tears streamed down Nan's face. "You really are fond of us? We aren't just a burden to you?"

"You have never been a burden to me. You both have worked so hard to pay your way and it has been pleasant to have you to talk to and fish with and all the chores have been a site more pleasurable…"

In spite of the attack, Nan felt happier than she could remember feeling since her parents died. Things were looking more positive. Elmer was going to see a doctor, Fred loved her a little, and she loved Fred too. Even the baby coming, scary as it was, was going to be all right. A small smile curved her lips.

Fred turned to look at her and saw the smile and his heart was glad. Elmer was sleeping soundly and the horse was making good time in the snow. They should make camp for noon and give the horse a rest. Nan probably needed rest too. He would have to be more attentive about that from now on.

"Here is a good place. I will get some firewood and we will make a little camp right here." Fred tied off Sonny and Ruby to a sapling, helped Elmer down, and then Nan. He got a little feed out of the saddlebag and gave it to the horse and mule. Elmer staggered and grabbed at his head with a moan. Nan quickly put her hand to his brow and felt the intense heat. "Fred, he is burning up!"

Elaine Littau

"Nan put some snow in this kerchief and I'll tie it to his head."

Nan returned with the snow filled kerchief and handed it to Fred. She ran to get one of the bedrolls off the back of the saddle. Fred spread it out and placed Elmer gently on the blanket, and Nan brought her bedroll for his head to lie on.

"I put a little soup in an old canteen. Let's heat it up and see if Elmer can sip a little. He needs to keep up his strength. I will get the fire going. You hold his head and comfort him. He needs his sister."

Nan cried uncontrollably when she looked at the pale face lying in her lap. He looked so weak and white. "Honey, please hold on. We are going to see a doctor that can help you get well. You can't give up!"

Elmer's eyes opened slightly and she saw the fear in them. "I don't know if I can hold on, Sissy. I am so tired. Don't be a'scared; Fred will take care of you if I die. He promised that he would help me take good care of you."

"You are doing a good job, sweet brother, but I need you to try to hold on. You are all I have left of Ma and Papa and our wonderful life together! Go to sleep for a few minutes and then you will have to drink some of this soup that Fred is putting on the fire."

Elmer closed his tired little eyes and struggled into a fitful sleep. Nan squeezed her eyes shut and gritted her teeth, "Don't you dare take him from me, God! Haven't I suffered enough? Hasn't he suffered enough? Are You even there? How can I believe in Someone Who has never been there for me? You let this happen to him! You let those men use me! Where were you?"

Fred heard her whispering hoarsely. She was almost growling. He had never seen her face so animated in anger. He ran to her side fearing the worst. No, Elmer was sleeping fitfully. He was at least alive. "What is it, Nan?"

"I can't talk to you about it."

"What is it?"

"No, I don't want preached at right now!"

"Why would I preach at you?"

"No! I ain't telling you nothin'!"

"What are you so mad about?"

"All right!…God. I am mad about or at God!…If there really is a God."

"How can you say that, Nan?"

"He has allowed nothin' but trouble in my life, and poor little Elmer too! I would hate to think that I would have to 'worship' Someone so cruel and mean."

"God is Sovereign, Nan. That means that He is in control and…"

"That's just it!" Nan growled. "If He is in control, why does He want to hurt us so much? I cannot stand it if Elmer dies! I really cannot go on living without him!"

"Let me pray for him again."

"No! God knows he needs help. If He wants to help, He will do it, but I don't think He gives a lick what happens to any of us."

"Nan!"

"Isn't that soup burning now?"

Fred went to the fire and the soup was boiling over. He put a small amount into a tin cup and brought it over to the sleeping boy. "Elmer, son, wake up and drink a little of this good ole soup. I made it just for you."

Elmer put his lips to the cup, but it was just too hot to drink. Fred got up from his crouched position and paced the camp with the little cup in his hand. He was struggling in his spirit also. "Lord, why is this happening? I want them to trust You and You keep letting things like this happen. I understand why Nan is questioning me about You. I have asked the same questions over and over in my own mind about Claire, Joy…and Elmer…also Nan. Why do you give me people to care for if You are going to cause them to suffer and die all the time?" He felt the all too familiar silent scream in his heart.

Nan thought he would preach to her about her questions. He had a plenty of his own. He had no idea what to say to her, except the little sentence that his Ma and Pa repeated over and over to him. *God is Sovereign and He is in control.* That gave him little comfort then and even now. Somehow though, it reached him those years ago when Claire and Joy died, that God really was in control of everything. The soup was getting cooler so he took his spot next to Elmer and offered it to the sick little one. He sipped ever so slowly, and then swallowed. His blonde hair was pasted on his head with perspiration. It was winter and snow was on the ground, but he had a high fever. Fred wrapped him in the bedroll and rocked him slowly while he urged more of the warm substance into his mouth. This little one must not die!

A twig snapped in the clearing and Fred looked up from his careful watch of the boy. There stood four Indians. He recognized one of them as his friend. He had called him James because he could not pronounce his Ute name. "James, I am glad to see you! Who do you have with you?"

"Fred, my friend, do you have trouble?"

"Yes, the boy is very sick. He has suffered headaches and fever many days for years."

"Then, it is not the sickness that comes and goes away fast, killing many."

"No. I am sure of that. He has been sick for three years."

"I will give to him some herbs for pain I use."

"Thank you, my friend."

"What are you thinking? He can't just give Elmer something! He might kill him!" Nan stood in front of Elmer with her arms crossed.

"Who is this little girl?" questioned a startled James.

"This is my wife, Nan."

"Wife? She is too young. I will give you my sister. This one is a baby."

Nan stretched to her fullest height and looked at James with a stern expression, "The boy is my brother and I say *no*."

"Is Fred your husband?"

"Yes."

"Then I do what he says. He is boss."

"What?" Nan turned to look at Fred and see his reaction.

"You heard him. I am the boss. Besides, their medicine really does work wonders."

"How is it that you explain yourself to a woman?'

"She is a new wife and doesn't know the ways of the wilderness."

"Better she learn fast."

"Yes, she will learn. I will explain and she will listen and learn."

"Good. If she doesn't learn her lessons well, remember I do have a sister that could be a good wife."

"I will keep that in mind, James."

Nan stood there unable to speak. She had escaped one boss to obtain another one. She wondered if he would take the law of the wilderness ways of beating wives into submission. She hadn't thought of that. Fred didn't seem to be that kind of man, but he spoke differently in front of these Indians. Would he get another wife? Was that legal? Maybe it was if one was an Indian. What would she do if that happened?

James reached into his shirt and pulled a leather thong from his neck. Attached to it was a small leather pouch with dried herbs in it. He took the tin cup Fred offered to him and placed a pinch of the herb into it. Fred put a little of the soup with it in the cup and placed the cup up to Elmer's lips. Elmer seemed oblivious to his surrounding and mechanically sipped the contents of the cup.

"It will make him sleep deep."

"Can we continue on the trail while he sleeps?"

"It is best if he is asleep while he travels, yes?"

"Thank you, my friend."

"You going to big settlement where your father lives?"

"Yes"

"God's speed to you."

"Go with God, James."

"Fred, a big preaching man is in the settlement of your father."

"Do you know him?"

"Yes, he is the one who is a close friend to you."

"Not Marcus Hall?"

"Brother Mark."

"Did you go to see him, James?"

"Yes, I also take these three brothers of mine. They see a difference in me and want to be like me."

"Are they like you now?"

"Yes, they take God as Holy Father of all, and His Son Jesus too."

"James, you...I don't know what to say! You helped me more ways than you know today."

"See, the boy sleeps in a resting way. You must go on now."

"Yes, we are going now."

Fred broke camp as soon as he could get things together. Nan held the peacefully sleeping Elmer close to her. She mused at the conversation that she witnessed between James and Fred. How was he a friend to Indians? Who was Brother Mark? Why would an Indian go to a church meeting, let alone take his brothers? There was a lot about Fred that she did not know. The medicine that James gave to Elmer gave him some peace and she was grateful for that.

"Come here, Nan. You get on first and I'll hand Elmer up to you."

Fred settled Elmer onto Nan's lap and they continued the descent down the mountain to the "big settlement" that Fred used to call home.

Chapter Sixteen

Mary could hardly believe her good fortune. She pressed the palms of her hands against her stomach and dreamed the dream of a childless woman with a glimmer of hope for a baby. She was to see the town doctor today to confirm her suspicions. It was a luxury, but she did not want to take any chances at her age. After all, she was thirty-two years old and not a spring chicken any more. Carefully she placed her newest hat upon her head and tilted it in the latest fashion. All the special pains in her grooming must be kept up to be reputed to be a respectable, somewhat prosperous, upstanding name in the community. There was no telling who she might run into in the mercantile. She had won respectability among the ladies in her church sewing circle and bridge club, but one could not be too careful or let their guard down. Mr. Dewey had even consented to attend the large fashionable church on the urging of Mary as to the importance of social standing in the small community. He had made a decent impression and it had boosted her endeavors tremendously. Sam had told her that he was glad that she had taken to the thought of making the Dewey name revered in the community. After all, Campo was growing and now was the time to be known as an established family. He wanted only the best for his children. Being respected and having children were about the only thing Mary could think of that Sam actually cared much about. Maybe when he was married to Nancy he knew he could never measure up to her perfect dead husband. Well, one thing was for sure, Mary came from hardy stock and bearing children was the one thing her mother did best. A smile flickered across Mary's lips as she remembered the five healthy brothers that were in her family. Mom had only lost two to childbirth. She knew of no one else in her hometown that could boast of that.

Elaine Littau

She pinched her cheeks and climbed into the buckboard that Sam had brought around to the front of the barn. She just knew that she would have good news to share today.

Sam waited outside the mercantile for Mary to finish up with the doctor. A lot depended on the news that she would have for him. If she were with child there was a fifty/fifty chance that by spring planting time his inheritance would be given to him. He only wished that he could know if the off-spring would be male. Sam was not a patient man, but there was nothing that could be done but wait it out. What would he do if it were a blamed female? Nothing he could do but try again and again if need be. Mary was strong. Some would have thought him crude if they knew that he had looked her over like a horse in an auction. He had learned his lesson with the pretty wife. For all his trouble he had ended up with a slew of dead babies and a dead wife who had left behind two off-spring of another man for him to deal with. He was glad they were gone. The townspeople would have expected him to treat them as if they were his own flesh and blood. Oh well, one thing Nancy left him was a big piece of property with a large house and barn, probably the best spread around these parts. He chewed these thoughts around in his head just like he was chewing on the long strip of jerky in his mouth while he leaned against the post waiting for that confounded woman. He turned his thoughts this way and that. There was one thing for sure; he certainly didn't have this woman figured out. When he left to see about Ma, she was meaner than a cougar. Now she was sweet as pie. He enjoyed the sparring of comments and the game of deceit. He knew that she was being deceitful, but at least she looked better, smelled better and cooked better than before. He didn't care much for the socializing part, but it did make sense to build a good reputation for his heirs. If it killed him, he would sit in that big, old, dusty church so he could be considered respectable. One thing made it bearable and that was that the Bible was hardly ever opened except for extremely familiar verses that seemed disconnected from his life. Mostly the parson spoke on politics and literature. There was some talk of a new man filling the position; hopefully he would be of the same temperament as the last fellow. Church attendance couldn't help but refine a man. His boy would be the best scholar money could buy. Some churches he had heard tell of were very emotional. Emotion has no place in a decent man's religion. Maybe the heathen Indians needed emotion, but not Sam Dewey!

Yonder a comin' it was Mary. Was it good news?

Mary looked quietly into the reflection in the mirror next to the washstand. She lit the lamp and peered deeply into the blue eyes looking back at her. Mary Dewey was expecting a baby. She had the luxury of time since Mr. Dewey went to the town saloon to celebrate the good news. She had all the time in the world. She was looking for something that had been missing for a long time. Yes, there it was, a sparkle reached the cornflower blue orbs and lit up the usually passive face. She placed her hand on the mirror and spoke softly to herself as she had in childhood days.

"Mary, can you believe it? You will finally have a family of your own. Little Mary, someone will really love you, and you will be free to love...him? Her? What did it matter, she would love with total abandon. What was that? Fear? Don't be afraid, Mary. You can handle anything. You are just like your Ma. She took care of all of you and did a fine job of it. No, I don't want to be just like Ma. I want to cuddle and kiss my babies. I want to devote myself to love." Her mind went quickly to Lester. Why did her stupid brain have to think of him at a time like this? Her eyes sparkled and danced with a shimmer on the night he asked her to be his wife. She had never known such happiness in her young life. Seventeen was the last year that a girl had "the flower of her youth" and she would be married before it had passed. She had worked so

Elaine Littau

hard on her wedding dress and the trousseau. The wedding was to have been the next day. Uncle Pete had knocked on the door and Ma had answered. He bore the news that his youngest frivolous daughter had run off with Lester. From that time on Mary had been a changed woman. Even as an eighteen year old, she put on the mantle of old maid. No one could reach the cold, scarred and broken heart.

For a moment the spark faded and the dead-pan look returned. She placed her hand on her stomach and remembered the life and love that was promised to be and a small light flickered inside the tortured soul and through the eyes. She was so glad to have this time to absorb her news without the prying eyes of Mr. Dewey. If he knew her heart wounds were still sore, he would delight in putting her in her place. She learned a very important lesson as of late. He wouldn't hit her if she were with child or if she remained interesting and kept them in public places where bruises could be observed. She would beat him at this game. She had grown to enjoy the challenge of outwitting him. He only thought it was his idea to have a child. It had been in her plans from the start. One important observation she had made was that he had no respect for pain or discomfort. He ranted and raved about his first wife Nancy and how fragile she had been. At first Mary had thought that he loved Nancy's delicate ways, and then she realized that it had only made him loathe her. If she were to fight him toe to toe, she would have to be strong, never complain, out work, and outwit him. She would be stoic in childbirth no matter what.

With that in mind she determined to not show one sign of weakness as long as she lived. The strange smile glided across her face and she turned to start the preparations for a hearty supper.

Mr. Dewey stepped into the kitchen and smelled the aroma of beans, cornbread, gravy, and coffee. His stomach growled as he lowered himself into a chair at the table. Mary looked almost pretty. She was smiling and handed him a cup of steaming coffee. He was a little drunk and needed the warm beverage to help him clear his mind.

"Mary, Honey, yer purdy tonight."

"Mr. Dewey, you don't say?"

"Mere, Sweetie, give Daddy a little kiss?"

"Okay, Daddy, then you have to eat your supper."

Mr. Dewey hungrily devoured her face in an energetic kiss and pulled her to his lap. Mary put her arms tightly around his neck and held him for dear life. It wasn't love, but it was something. Something was better than nothing.

"Here, Daddy, eat your supper while it is hot. I'll kiss you again later."

Sam laughed heartily. "Sure thing, little Mama, it smells good."

Chapter Seventeen

Nate and Martha were sitting at the dinner table eating the noon meal when they heard the scraping of boots on the back porch. "Land sakes Nate, who could that be?"

"Well lookie here, it's our Fred and the younguns! Hey, boy, what are you doing in these parts? Is everything alright?"

Martha noticed the small boy sleeping in Fred's arms. Little Elmer was painfully white and still. "Fred honey, what is wrong? Bring that child in here and lay him on the little bed in the front bedroom. Let me turn down the covers! Oh mercy me, he looks bad!"

Martha made short work of preparing the child for rest under her clean covers in the small bed. Turning a quick eye to Nate, she instructed so gently yet urgently, "Dad, we must get the doctor in here to look at the little feller. Can you go fetch him, please?...And Papa take care of their animals!"

"Surely Mother, I will make haste. Fred sit there and take a rest. My goodness Nan, you better sit down too! What happened to you children?"

"Papa, I'll see to them, just get the doc as soon as he can get here!"

Martha felt the fevered brow and hurriedly went into the kitchen. Fred and Nan heard her rustling around the kitchen getting water from the pump, but both were exhausted and glued to the spot. In no time Martha returned to the small brightly colored room and administered a cool wet cloth to the patient. When she was satisfied that the child was breathing a fraction more easily, she looked into the faces of her precious son and the girl that sat next to him. "Children, come to the kitchen table and I'll get you some sustenance. You look beat."

Meekly they followed her to the table, which was set for two. "I'll get a couple of plates and get you some of this stew. I wondered why I made so much of this today, but I guess God knew that I would have family in today. I think I will make a little potato soup for Elmer...yes, that might set better in his little tummy. Don't you think? Oh listen to me chattering, Fred, you and Nan can go ahead and start. Papa already asked the blessin.' Land sakes let me get some milk and more bread put on. Lord knows I'm so glad to see you."

Obediently the two travelers quietly started eating the hearty dinner. Nan decided that she had never tasted anything so warm and comforting. She wished in her heart that she would not ever be required to speak while she was here. It was so healing just to hear Martha fussing over them and the one-sided banter made her feel that she could really rest and not have to think.

Martha stopped in mid sentence, "Fred, what is wrong with Elmer?"

Fred wiped his mouth with the cloth napkin from his lap and cleared his throat. "Ma, he is hurting so bad. His head has been hurting without stopping for days. I had to get him here to see a doctor. I'm even thinking that I might take him to Denver if I don't get answers here."

"How is he able to sleep when he is in such pain?"

"We ran into James on the trail and he gave us some herbal medicine for him."

"I don't know, Fred..." Martha's voice trailed off, "but I guess sleep is better than pain."

Nan tore the bread at her plate and dreaded answering any questions that Martha might ask of her. She savored the luscious stew and felt strength flow into her tired body. Maybe if she didn't look Martha in the eye, Martha would continue speaking with Fred."

"Nan dear, you look all done in. I think you need to get into bed soon."

"Thank you, but I want to see what the doc says about Elmer and I really need to check on him."

"I know, dear. That is a sweet sister."

Presently the doctor and Nate entered the sick room. Dr. Benson felt for the pulse and made a mental note of it. Then he listened to the small chest and felt the fevered brow.

"This boy has a major infection somewhere in his body. Some doctors still hold to the practice of bleeding the patient to relieve the body of impurities, but my Ma was what people called a healer back in the hills of Kentucky and she swore that she saw more people die of the bleedin' than it helped. What kind of herbs did you say you gave him to help him to sleep?"

"My friend from the Ute tribe gave them to Elmer. Here is the bag. It still has some herbs in it."

Doc Benson dipped his fingers into the small leather pouch and procured a pinch of herbs between his forefinger and thumb. Rubbing them together, he bent his head to sniff, "Peers to be the same type of folk medicine my Ma uses. I don't see any harm coming from it. In fact, it may be just the ticket to get this lil guy some rest." Carefully he examined the sleeping boy. "I need to look down his throat and see if it is festered in there. Sometime the tonsils don't bide well with children. Fred, can you hold his head and prop his mouth open a little? Mercy, would you look at that! How long did you say the little feller has been poorly?"

Nan spoke firmly, "Since he was three years old. He is nigh onto six now."

"He has a festered tooth. The poison has spread to the roof of his mouth. His tooth socket in the back there is just about gone. It looks to have been broken off jagged like. Did he have a bad fall or something?"

Nan thought for a moment. She recalled the time Mr. Dewey had Elmer go to the pasture with him to check on a cow that was ripe to deliver her calf. When Elmer got back his face was very red on the jaw and Mr. Dewey had said that the cow kicked him. Nan found out later that Mr. Dewey had backhanded the toddler. Anger consumed her as the memory flooded back. "Only the backhand of a hateful man."

Doc Benson looked quickly at Fred. Martha piped up, "No, not our Freddy. It was a stepfather years ago!"

"However it happened, the poison has to be expressed. If much of it gets to his stomach, it could kill him."

"What are you going to do?" Nan spat out.

"Well, let's see here. I don't cotton to bleedin' folks, but he needs to bleed clean after I lance the festered part. I'm gonna use a few leeches to do the job." The doctor grabbed his bag and fished out a pile of clean rags. "I aim to pack his mouth with these to catch the poison when I lance this thing. Martha, get me some more to replace these because I have a feeling these will soak up fast. Nate, go to my office and get the jar of leeches in my window. Bring them fast. Fred, hold his head still."

With a small sharp knife in his hand, the man of medicine plunged the blade into the festered mouth, slicing through the tender skin from the back tooth to the roof of Elmer's mouth. Martha was amazed at how quickly the first rags filled with the foul fluid. The smell was horrendous. Nan ran out the door and lost all her dinner. She continued to wretch throughout the surgery. Time after time the putrid rags were replaced with clean ones. Finally, when the rags were a bright red instead of the putrid yellow and green, Doc Benson reached into the jar and selected two leeches to do "clean up" work. He monitored them as they each grew fat on blood. He returned them to the jar and fetched two more. After they gorged themselves, he put them back into the jar and packed the last of the clean rags into Elmer's mouth. He turned to speak to the worried attendees, "I am going to have to try to pull that stub of a tooth. I reckon he will come to when I try to do this so I have a plan. I am going to knock him out."

Nan sucked in her breath, "Why would you do that?"

"Just trust me little lady. It has to be done."

"You ain't gonna hit him are you?"

"No. Nate, get me a hammer and Martha, bring me a big cast iron cooking pot. I will put the pot on his head and hit it with the hammer and it will put him out."

"Doc, are you shore?" Nate stroked the stubble on his chin and looked stern with his brow furrowed in deep lines, "Couldn't it kill him?"

"Yes, it could kill him if it ain't done just right, but I have done the knock out before and the old drunk I did it to lived to tell about it. I couldn't give the old codger enough whiskey to put him out for the operation, so I had to knock 'em out."

"Is it wise to do that to a young child?" Martha couldn't stand the thought or the risk.

"Martha, we don't have a choice. We got rid of a bunch of poison, but the cause of the poison is that fractured tooth and jaw. I will have to chip out all the pieces of fractured jaw too. It should heal up and give him a lot of relief."

When the doctor knocked out Elmer he hurriedly removed the blood soaked rags and found the piece of tooth embedded into the gums. With small pliers, he grabbed it and it slipped. After many tries, he held the offending bit of tooth in the grip of the pliers. He removed many small pieces of bone from the jaw and the blood poured. The doctor was worried about the enormous amount of blood that the child had lost, but there was nothing he could do about that. After much time had passed the old doc declared the operation to be over. He heated a small bit of iron over a coal oil lamp until it turned red and seared the wounds inside the mouth of the patient. That was the only way to get the blood to stop flowing. Hopefully the little boy would live.

He hollered at Martha, "Martha, you better do your best prayin' now cause I've done all I can. It is up to the good Lord to bring him through now. He is going to hurt something awful when he comes to. Just give him more of that Injun medicine and he can stand it. Could I have some coffee? I'm stayin' until I see that he wakes up from the knock out."

Nan was standing at the door and the doc almost knocked her down on his way to the dinner table to drink the coffee.

"Kid, you need to get some rest. Martha, get this girl in bed now. Her brother will be out for a while. She don't need to watch him sleep."

Fred took three long strides and was at Nan's side. He scooped her up and carried her to his old room. He put her down beside the bed and ordered her to remove her travel clothes. As she removed them, he dug into the pack and found her nightdress. Keeping his back to her he handed her the garment. "Put this on and climb under the covers, Nan."

She obediently climbed under the covers and lie there. The exhaustion of the day came down upon her and her lips were parched. Fred looked down upon the small figure and noticed the chapped lips. "I'll bring you a drink of water if you want."

"Thank you."

As carefully as a mother with a newborn, Fred held the dipper of water to her lips and watched her take in a few gulps. Gently he laid her back onto her pillows and tucked her in. Without forethought he bent and kissed her delicate brow. The cool brow startled him to reality and he started to apologize for the gesture, but the recipient was sleeping soundly.

Martha was standing in the doorway and took in the tender scene. She couldn't help but be concerned by the way her son was behaving. True, he treated the girl kindly, but there was more to it than she felt ought to be. "Fred, what is going on? You have changed. Come in here and tell me about it."

The last thing Fred felt like doing was telling his parents, not to mention the doctor, that he and Nan were married. It was probably better to tell them today while Nan was sleeping than to have them searching her face while the tale was told.

"Yes, Ma and Pa, Doc Benson, I do have some news.'

"Well…"

"Ma, a few months ago Nan told me that she is sixteen years old. I knew that if word got out that she had been living in the wilderness with a widower, it would ruin her reputation so I decided to marry her."

"Son, do you mean to tell me that you love this child?" Nate queried.

"I care for her very much, but love is…You know there will never be another Claire."

"Are you telling us that Nan is sixteen years old? Fred, were you improper with her? Is that the basis of this marriage?" Martha's voice was wooden and small.

"Mother, Nan and I were not intimate before our marriage. However, just so that you know, she is with child. She conceived on the week we were wed."

"Just where did you go to get married son?" Nate asked.

"Silverton. Like I said, when I realized her age, I knew that the old hens of our town would be unkind to her and her reputation would be ruined. Besides, Nan and Elmer still need protection from those stepparents. This way, they cannot touch them since Nan is my wife."

Doctor Benson rubbed the gray stubble on his chin thoughtfully, "Has Nan been feeling alright since the marriage and the baby on the way?"

"She has been worried sick about Elmer. She doesn't sleep most nights because she checks on him constantly. It is good to see her sleeping so soundly now."

"Probably relief. Elmer should recover nicely if he makes it through the night. He had a passel of poison in his system and he isn't out of the woods yet."

"He hasn't spoken much for a few days. The pain was too much for him. It was a relief when James gave us the herbs to help him sleep. Nan was afraid he was dying."

"Well, Fred, if you would have waited another day or two, it might have been too late. But about Nan, take good care of her. She is too thin and her color is bad. She needs almost as much rest as Elmer. Do you understand?"

Martha assured them all. "I'll see to it that they get fat and sassy in no time."

"Good girl."

"Doc, you look like you are about to drop yourself. Why don't you rest a bit? I will sit with Elmer for a spell."

"I want to be here when he is conscious, but I believe I will go to the house for a couple of hours and get some shuteye. I will be back before sun up to relieve you."

"How can we ever thank you, Doc?" Fred had tears standing in his eyes.

"It isn't really over, boy, but I think it will be alright."

Nate took his watch over the tiny boy. Fred came into the room and placed his hand on his Dad's shoulder, "Dad, I don't ever want to do anything that would hurt you. You know that don't you?"

"Yes, my boy, I trust that you did what you felt God wanted you to do. In fact, I think this might be just the thing you needed to help you get back into life and the ministry."

"Let's not rush it. I don't know if I could ever stand in front of people again and preach."

"We'll see." Nate had a twinkle in his eye at the thought of hearing his boy preach again.

"Fred, I guess you can stay in the room with Nan since you are married now." Martha stood in the doorway hating to intrude on the hushed conversation, but knowing that her son was exhausted.

"I do feel the tiredness creeping up on me. I will be up in a while to check on Elmer. Let me know when he wakes up."

Fred crept into his old bedroom and saw that Nan had not moved one muscle since he had tucked her in. He had to mess up his side of the bed so that his folks wouldn't guess that there was more to their story. Fred eased himself carefully onto his side of the bed and lay there intending to get up with a blanket and sleep on the floor, but fatigue overtook him and he fell asleep as soon as his head hit the pillow.

"Fred, dear." The whisper of his mother's voice in his ear broke through the dreamless sleep of the exhausted man. "Elmer woke up. He has a little color to his complexion

Elaine Littau

now but he is really hurting. Can you give him the herbs? I didn't know how much to give to him...I'm sorry to disturb your rest."

"Quite alright, Mother." Fred was on his feet in an instant.

Elmer looked at Fred and tears were filling his large blue eyes. He parted his lips to speak but the pain from the lancing and cauterizing prevented words. Fred knelt down beside him and wrapped his arms around the small boy and comforted him. "You know, Elmer, if I could give you some of my strength, I would."

Elmer nodded gravely.

"My Lord can help you through this. He said that He is our strength when we are weak. He will do what He says. I believe it. Do you?"

Again Elmer nodded assent.

Fred placed his big muscular work hardened hand on Elmer's head and prayed a simple but moving prayer, "Jesus, You promised to never leave us or forsake us. My partner here feels pretty low and needs strength in his little body. Please make the healing come and bring health to Elmer. In Jesus' name, amen."

He put two pinches of the herbs in a small amount of cool water and mixed it together, "Here Pard, drink up. That's a good boy. Go back to sleep. I'll be right here standing guard over you."

The young one groaned and moaned for a few moments and was soon asleep. Fred sat in the old rocker his ma had placed in the room for those who kept watch. The familiar creak it made as he rocked gave him a strange feeling of comfort. The sound was homey and nostalgic of his childhood days. It brought memories of Dad sitting beside the fireplace and Mama in this very rocker during Scripture reading before bed flooded his mind. He spent a good many hours praying in this old rocker when the Lord had spoken to his heart about becoming a preacher. He thought about all those times while he kept a silent watch. Preaching was way down the list of things he wanted to do, although he did miss the connection he felt with God Almighty when he knew that the words he was speaking were the ones God had placed on his lips. Well, at any rate, it would take a real miracle for him to get back to preaching. He wasn't rushing into anything like that. Most likely parishioners would never change.

Fred was glad to see that a little color was coming into the deathly pale skin of the boy. Who would of thought that a broken tooth could endanger a life? He really was a little soldier to not whine and cry over it all the time. How much damage had Elmer and Nan suffered at the hands of those stepparents? He thought about Nan. He couldn't help but notice when he took her away from the trappers that her back was a mass of scars. Her back had virtually no smooth skin. Thinking of that day brought back the ugliness of what had happened. Poor little Nan, what would her life have been had her Mother and Father not died, Elmer too, for that matter. She would have probably been the smartest girl in the schoolhouse. Nan was sharp and learned quickly. There likely would have been a farmer's son who would have been trying to catch her eye. Somehow, it made Fred feel strange to think of Nan with someone else. She would have had several serious suitors. She really was quite pretty with that raven hair and those earnest brown eyes. She may not have been interested in those kinds of things yet had she had a happy life with her real parents. She seemed to be the "tomboy" type, strong and competitive. It was too bad that her childhood was stolen from her as it had. These thoughts turned in his mind for the hours that he kept the late night watch.

The boy tossed and turned as the dawn approached. The pain was evident on his face. He moaned loudly and began vomiting violently. Fred grabbed a clean cloth and dipped it into the cool water beside the bed and mopped Elmer's forehead with it. "Hang in there, Pard."

The doctor stepped quietly into the room. "Good job, Elmer. We need all that poison that got away from us to get out of your body. Don't fight it." Fred stepped away from the bed to allow the doc to get a closer look at Elmer. "Fred, go to bed. I am here now and if we are going to lick this thing, both of us had better take rest when we can."

Fred left the room with a silent nod of thanks. He was too tired to do anything but lie on his side of the bed and sleep. Sleep came immediately and the tired anguished mind was finally at peace.

The sun was shining brightly when Nan awoke. How long had she slept and where was Elmer? As she turned to climb out of the bed, she saw Fred lying there. Oh yes, he had to be there so that his parents wouldn't know that this was not a marriage born of love. Looking at the sound sleeper, she denied the term that indicated that love was not an issue in this marriage. Fred had a great love for her and Elmer. He was their shield from harsh gossip. He carefully explained to her about the talk that kills and wounds innocent people. He reassured her that she was innocent. She hadn't deserved to be hurt by those horrible men. It took a lot of talk and quite a bit of convincing for her to realize that she didn't deserve the pain and hurt that had come to her short life. The only way he could reach her to convince her of that was the argument that if she deserved her mistreatment, then surely Elmer deserved his. Why, he was a sweet little guy who had never hurt anyone! Fred convinced her that she was just as sweet and kind as Elmer. She watched Fred breath steadily in deep sleep. Fred was kind. She had no doubt about that. He loved her little brother and that was good enough for her. Although, there was something else that was intangible. She had the feeling that he did understand her, maybe better than she understood herself. He was lying on his side facing toward her. One arm was pillowing his head and the other was on top of the covers. His arms were bronze and muscular. She remembered walking up on him in the summer when he and Elmer were chopping wood. He had taken his shirt off. He was so embarrassed for her to see him bare-chested. He grabbed the cast-off garment quickly and shoved his arms into it in one motion, buttoning the front unevenly. She smiled at the remembrance. He had seemed more like a boy than man at the time. He had big strong hands. They were rough, but so tender whenever he tended to Elmer. That memory brought quick tears to her eyes. She and Elmer were lucky to have Fred. She determined that he would not be sorry that he had taken them on.

Nan noticed the black hair tossed onto his forehead, his straight nose, and gentle firm mouth. He still had a weary look around his eyes. Those bright blue eyes that twinkled merrily when he teased them could become daggers of fiery ice when anger came. She would like to be able to examine his eyes without his knowledge, just as she was looking at him now, because she did not want him to catch her. What would she do if the handsome face that she was peering at came to life as those big eyes opened? She would be mortified. What would she say?

She dragged her gaze off the sleeping man to the cozy room where they lay. Martha was warm and cozy like this room. Oh what was she thinking? Elmer. How was he doing? She must check on him at once. She quietly climbed out of the bed and wrapped a large shawl from the chair around her shoulders and made her way to the small room at the front of the house. Elmer was awake and looking a sight better. He was taking a little water. She could only imagine the pain in his mouth from the cauterizing of the wounds.

"Elmer honey, how are you feeling?"

"No headache," replied the raspy voice.

"No headache? Oh that is wonderful!"

"Nan, he can't speak much or it will cause the bleeding to start up again," said the doctor.

"I understand. I am so relieved that his headache has stopped."

"He has been resting quite well. I think that the healing will come fast as soon as he gets a little strength back. He had so much poison that it could have killed him if it had busted out by itself. He is quite blessed to have made it to surgery in time."

"What can I do for him?" she asked.

"You can get some rest. I know about the marriage and about the baby. You have to take good care of yourself, else you won't do anyone any good."

"When? How..." Nan put her hand to her throat.

"Fred told his ma, pa and me about it when you went to bed. He said that he wanted to keep people from gossiping about a sixteen-year-old girl living in the wilderness with him. I think there is more to it, but it looks like he did the right thing. Are you sure that you are sixteen, girl?"

"Yes, sir." Nan was so glad that Fred had told the news without her being present. She had never been a good liar.

"So the baby will he here around the last of May, right?"

"We got married the first part of October, wouldn't it be July?"

"Just checking," Grinned the doctor.

Nan blushed all the way to her toes and left the room.

Quietly Nan climbed into the feather bed. Fred had not moved since she left. Just as her head touched the soft pillow, the sleeper awoke. "Is everything alright, Nan? How is Elmer?"

"He was awake and said his head quit hurting!" Nan was batting back the tears that came to her eyes.

Fred quickly put his arms around her and gave her a bear hug. "Isn't that good news?" He was speaking with tears in his voice. He patted her on the back and stroked her hair as if she were a small child. He kissed her forehead and as his lips brushed past her hair, he became aware of the spontaneous embrace. She had laid her head on his shoulder and was quietly crying. "Nan, I'm sorry. I didn't intend to become so... familiar." The words stumbled through his lips.

"No Fred, I just can't believe that it is finally over for Elmer and he will be getting well. You have been good to us. I love how you care for us." She was sobbing great body- wracking sobs while she spoke.

"Let me get up and give you some time for yourself, Nan."

"No, please. Could you just hold me next to your heart? My Pa used to comfort me like that. I can't stop crying. I feel so stupid for crying because he will get well."

"You have been carrying a big burden for such a little girl. Just cry all you want and I'll hold you while you sleep. My heart breaks for you and all you have been through. I have to admit that I have been shedding grateful tears about Elmer too."

Somehow knowing that he felt the same about her little brother slowed the tears. She listened to the steady beating of his heart and slept peacefully.

Fred heard her sobs slow and finally the soft breathing of deep sleep was evident. This sweet girl-woman was his wife. He was not sorry about that. He was really attached to her. No, he had to admit to himself that he loved her and that he wanted her to love him as a husband. When could or would that ever happen? It felt so right to lie next to her. She was still torn up about the attack. He doubted that she would ever see him as a husband or herself as his wife. She stirred and he smelled the fragrance of her hair. It was a sweet, clean smell. She lay there so trusting in his arms.

He began to pray. "Lord, thank you for taking care of Elmer. I pray that you will help my little wife too. She has as much poison in her as Elmer did only it ain't the kind a doctor can get rid of. Heal us all. My own heart isn't where it ought to be with You, Lord. Show me what to do. In Jesus' Name. Amen." In a matter of moments he was engulfed in deep sleep also.

Chapter Eighteen

After a month of rehabilitation at Nate and Martha's, Elmer was well. The burns in his mouth had healed and the headaches had not returned. He had a few nights of careful attention from his family and the kind doctor, but he was as good as mended. As the three prepared to go back up to the cabin, Martha had to try to convince Fred to stay in town through the rest of the winter. "Fred, Nan needs to be here with me so that I can give her motherhood instructions. You don't want her giving birth all alone do you?"

"Mother, the babe won't be here until July. We will be back for the birth. We want to go home."

Many days of persuasion came and left and the little family was finally at the homestead. Nan hadn't realized how much she had missed the crisp snowy air of the high Rockies. The sight of the small cabin against the woods made her heart sing. She truly felt that she was at home. The trip back up the mountain was joyous. She had never heard Elmer talk so much. In fact, he was quite the chatterbox. He asked so many questions that she was sure Fred would scold him. Fred quietly answered every question. He was kind and patient with the inquisitive little boy. Actually, he was a really good teacher. Nan was learning a lot from listening to the conversation between the two. The questions Elmer asked were quite advanced for a young boy. Fred told him of the geology of the rocky crags and formations that miners watched for to find silver and gold. One lesson was of the vegetation on the slopes that they traversed. As they stopped in front of the cabin Elmer asked, "Fred, will eating raw eggs kill a body?"

Nan had to suppress a smile at the remembrance of the train ride.

"Elmer, I am sorry to say that everyone who has ever eaten an egg raw or cooked has died."

The look on Fred's face was grave.

"Really?" Nan gasped.

"Yep, eventually everybody dies!"

Elmer was the first to burst into gales of laughter.

"I should hit you...I don't know what to say to you!" yelled Nan.

"What's the matter? I was just joshing with you!"

"Nan is mad 'cause you scared her. She made me eat raw eggs on the train and she even ate some too."

"Why did you two eat raw eggs?"

"We was starvin' and my stomach hurt almost as much as my head. Mrs. Dewey didn't like for us to eat too much."

"I'm sorry to bring back a bad memory for you two. Forgive me, Nan."

"I will have to think on that for a spell. Forgiveness too quick is cheap. You will think that scaring a body is too easy to get forgiveness for."

"Nan, you need to forgive me for your sake as much as for mine."

"I don't see how that would affect me at all for you to not be forgiven by me," snorted Nan.

"Unforgiveness is like that festered tooth of Elmer's. At first it just smarts a little and then if left alone it could poison your whole mind and life."

"Just give me a little time to think about that. I think that if I don't forgive you, it will hurt you a little and I won't feel anything. Just let me be."

"You will see that I am right."

"You bet. You are always right aren't you?!" Nan scrambled off the horse and made for the creek.

"She won't be mad long. She never stays mad at me." Elmer patted his friend on the arm to comfort him.

Fred watched her trudge through the shin deep snow. "I guess some things have to be lived out before people believe what you preach to them."

"Were you preachin,' Fred? Is that what preachin' is?"

Fred had to laugh when he saw the comical look of concern on Elmer's face. "Yep, Pard, I guess I was. Sorry."

Why did things that Fred say grate against her nerves? Sometimes she wanted to hug him, but most of the time she felt like beating him on the chest with her firsts. She had never felt like doing anything like that to anyone in her life. What was the matter with her? She felt like she was living in someone else's skin. The skin didn't fit her. It was too tight and she couldn't breathe. All the hurt that she had suffered was coming to her mind and wanting to burst out of her lips. She hated the indignities she suffered at the hands of others, yet she found herself thinking thoughts of venom. She was glad that she hadn't said most of the things that had come into her mind. Forgiveness? Never! A thousand times never! From this day on she would protect herself and those she loved from frightening things, even if it were just stupid jokes. Allow someone to hurt you just a little and then the real pain will start. No. She vowed never to forgive anyone again.

After a few moments, she was chilled to the bone. Quietly she entered the cabin; Fred and Elmer were bedding down the horses and mule. She took a seat in the low rocker in front of the open fireplace. Fred had started a small fire and it was popping noisily. She needed to start the cornbread, but she was exhausted and stayed seated. The flames eagerly licked the dry logs and brought forth needed warmth to the small room. She placed her feet on a small stool next to the hearth and allowed herself to completely relax. Before long her eyes were too heavy to remain open. She felt strong arms lift her and carry her to the big bed that she and Elmer shared. The covers were icy cold, but a heated rag-covered stone was placed at her feet and she felt cozy and warm. As she drifted more deeply to sleep she wondered why Fred was always so good to her. She had been hateful and mean. He never lost patience with her or struck her in anger. What was she going to do?

Early the next morning she heard the usual sounds of Fred doing chores. The axe rang clear in the yard with the splintering of the logs as they were first halved then quartered. He must have been up a while because the chopping of wood was toward the last of morning chores. He must have already fed the Sonny and Ruby. Dear me, Nan thought, "I am supposed to take care of the chickens and milk the cow." Fred insisted that they get them before they left Trinidad so that she and Elmer would have milk and eggs. Those confounded eggs! Why did I have to get so mad about that stupid joke! Hurriedly she dressed and headed to the small log barn.

Fred saw her as she walked briskly from the cabin. *I surely do hope she is over her mad spell,* he thought. As she drew near to the wood stack she cast her gaze to the ground, "Fred, I got riled up over nothin.' I guess my feelings are tender now…I'm sorry. You have been good to us and I want to try to behave myself."

"You are a good girl, Nan. Even when you get mad it doesn't change the fact that you are good. It might make it a little tough to see your natural sweetness, but it is still there. It was a stupid attempt at a joke and I am the one who is sorry. Let's have a good day, okay? I already milked and fed the cow, but the chickens haven't been fed yet."

Nan smiled and walked through the barn door and found a tin bucket on a nail by the door. Under it was a sack of chicken feed. The sack had bright pink flowers on it. It reminded her of the chore dress her Mama had worn and she smiled. She carefully pulled the loosely sewn string that closed the top of the sack and stuck her hand in to get a few handfuls of feed to put in the bucket. The big old Jersey cow that stood in a stall next to Sonny and Ruby lowed a welcome to her. Elmer named her Bobby because her tail had been bobbed off after a wild dog bit it half off when she was a calf. After looking around the barn she stepped into the yard and looked to see

Elaine Littau

where Fred had put the chickens. "They are in the old chicken house around the back of the barn."

"Old chicken house? You mean the storage shed?"

"It was a chicken house before Claire and Joy died, but I turned it into storage because I just couldn't take care of anyone or anything properly after…I took the things that were in there and put them in the barn in the crates we brought the chickens in. I don't know what I will do with those things."

Nan didn't ask him what they were. She already knew that they were probably personal items of his family. He must have had a hard morning doing that type of work. She edged around the barn and opened the door to the small chicken house. Even though the sun was shining, it was pretty cold out with snow on the ground. She looked at them and decided that they were beautiful. Yes beautiful! They were black with white speckles all over them. The rooster was spectacular to look at. Fred said they were called Barred Plymouth Rock. They also got some Guineas to warn them of predators lurking about. They gratefully took the feed that she scattered on the floor of the chicken house. She decided to put some feed in an old tin plate and filled a bowl with water. She didn't want them outside yet.

Elmer slept an hour or so longer than Nan had. He stood in the door of the cabin and stretched as far as his body would go. He was growing quickly now. They celebrated his sixth birthday with Nate and Martha. The cake had been delicious. Martha taught Nan how to make many dishes and she enjoyed the instruction on making that special cake most of all. Mainly because the celebration would not have taken place at all if the doctor hadn't done the surgery on him in time. Nan observed him as he scampered across the yard to Fred.

Elmer called out, "Fred, are we going to check your traps today? I bet you have caught a lot since we have been gone so long."

"Yes, we are going and I have a special treat for the two of you today. Nan is going to join us and we are going to a real Ute village. I want you to meet James' family."

"Are you certain that it is alright for us to go there?" Nan had heard many bad things about Indians and was not anxious to get too close for too long to them.

"James is a remarkable Christian man. You will enjoy meeting his family."

Nan remembered that James was trying to give Fred his sister as a wife and wasn't sure that she agreed.

After eating a quick breakfast, Fred brought Ruby and Sonny around for them to ride. He walked along side of them. The camp wasn't very far, but they would take it slow for Nan's sake. She was in her fifth month of pregnancy. She was beginning to show her condition and because of it he took special pains to be certain not to push her very hard. By noonday they were at the edge of the camp. Nan observed the children running after little pups and the women tending fires outside the teepees. They were obviously tending fires inside them too as smoke curled up through the posts at the top. The people stopped their activities and gathered at the side of the visitors.

"Greetings, friends! I brought my family to meet you."

Out of the crowd a familiar face approached Fred. "It is a good day to see my brother, Fred."

"I agree, James. You remember my family?"

James strode up to Elmer and peered into his glowing face. "This one looks much stronger than the last time I saw him."

"That's Elmer. He couldn't have made it if you hadn't helped him. I wanted to come and show you how well he has fared."

"Did you find the cause of his sickness?"

"It was a poisoned tooth that had broken off in the back of his mouth."

"Simple things can cause death."

"Yes."

"Your wife is of a better temperament it seems."

"Yes, Nan feels much happier since her brother is well."

"Nan, I am James. I welcome you to our camp."

"Thank you."

James led them to his comfortable home. The floor was cushioned on the perimeter with hides of deer, buffalo and many other pelts. A young woman was stirring a pot of stew-like substance cooking over a low flame. She looked up and smiled at Fred. "Hello, brother! It is good to see you after such a long time. Is this the wife my husband told me about?"

"Nan, this is New Moon, the wife of James."

The woman looked amused, "Fred could never get his mouth around our native tongue so he gave us the names he could say. My name and my husband's name are very difficult for the white man to say so we accept the ones that Fred gave us. Fred, what meaning does your name have?"

Fred laughed heartily, "Nothing, absolutely nothing. I don't know many white people with a name that means anything!"

"What a waste! Our names are given to us in remembrance of something or someone or to help us live up to great feats."

"I am named in remembrance of my mother. Her name was Nancy and so is mine. I just am called Nan."

"That is good."

James took Fred and Elmer outside while Nan visited with New Moon. Elmer quickly made friends with some of the children of the camp. "Fred, I want to give you some gifts for being my good friend."

"I couldn't take anything more from you, James. You have been a good friend ever since you came to my church in Trinidad and gave your life to the Lord. You stood by me when I fell into sin and helped me get out of it. Of all the people in the world, you have been my truest friend and brother."

They spied Elmer playing with some of the boys who had a litter of wolf pups. He was laughing at their wrestling and snipping at each other. "James, if you would like to give me something, I do need a dog now. Maybe one of those pups?"

"What happened to Rufus?"

"An intruder killed him."

"Indian?"

"No, trapper."

James called out to the boys in his native tongue, "Little brothers, help Elmer choose a pup. One that will grow up strong and loyal."

One of the boys handed a reddish-blonde pup to Elmer. He was part wolf, part husky because he was fathered by Rufus. The young boy spoke in broken English to Elmer, "I call him Shasta for a great mountain in the north that a white man who came to our camp told me about."

"Shasta! What a great name. Thank you James!" Elmer couldn't remember a day that he had been this happy. The little pup licked him as he laughed and wrestled with him.

"Now we will get a horse for Nan," said James.

"You have done too much already, James."

"I give a gift to the bride of my friend." James spoke softly as he handed the reins to Nan. She was overwhelmed as she looked at the beautiful appaloosa mare. It was black with white splotches on its hindquarter. What a horse!

"She is the tamest horse I own. She will serve you well. I call her Moon Shadow but you may call her what you wish."

"Moon Shadow is perfect! How can I thank you enough, James?"

"Just make my friend happy. Treat him well and be a good wife to him. Is that a bargain?"

"I will do my best." Somehow the exchange between James and her felt more like giving a marriage vow than the pitiful ceremony in Silverton did. "I will."

Fred smiled and knew that she had truly vowed to be his wife this time.

Nan enjoyed watching Fred as he planed the boards to make a large cradle for the baby. He said that it should be good-sized so that the child could use it for a couple of years. That made sense. The wood curled as it was planed from the board. It reminded Nan of Elmer's curls when he was a toddler. She smiled at the thought. The baby was kicking a lot these days. She could swear

Elaine Littau

that he felt that her belly was a drum that needed to be pounded night and day. Lately the baby had been stretching or something. She seemed to not be able to sit tall enough to give him enough room. She stood as much as possible, but it made her very tired. Fred had made her recline in the bed after dinner and in the evening time. She was embarrassed to be in the bed in the middle of the day. What would people think of her? She did it because it was the only way she could seem to relax these days. She had given up on ever seeing her feet again. It was a good thing that she had moccasins because her feet were too swollen for the high-topped boots she usually wore. Even at that Elmer or Fred had to help her get them on. She felt awkward and helpless. Fred said that they would go down to Trinidad at the end of this month so that she would have a month to get settled there before the baby came. If she had a little more than a month to go, how big was she going to be by the time she delivered? How big would the baby be? Nan was frightened. She tried to hide her concern and concentrated on watching Fred construct the cradle. Elmer was laughing in the distance. He was training Shasta to fetch a stick. They were inseparable. It was good to see him so happy and healthy.

"I'm going to start packing up the cabin in a few days. We will load the animals down with our household goods and prepare to move from the mountain for good."

Nan frowned, "For good?"

"It is time for me to face the world again. Elmer needs to attend school and you will want to be near civilization when the baby comes."

"We won't live here anymore?"

"No. I...we must go back home to Trinidad. Ma and Pa were anxious about you being up here when they found out that you were having a baby."

Nan remembered and nodded.

"We will take as much of our things as possible when we go, but I imagine I will be coming to clear the rest of the things here for setting up our own home in Trinidad."

Chapter Nineteen

Like a viper winding its way through the cracks and crags of the rock outcroppings, a man of slight build gazed down at the little cabin in the clearing. He stayed downwind of the small dog. He didn't want the critter to catch scent of him before he had time to load his gun and take aim. A smirk crossed the young dirty face and traces of tobacco juice slipped down the corner of his mouth. Dan was out for revenge. That preacher man had a lot of nerve killing his pa like that. *So what if we took the girl. She wasn't all that much. Shoot, they thought she was a boy before the kid yelled her name out.* A sly smile widened across his leathery face. She was a girl. The first white girl he had ever taken. His eyes scanned the property around the barn and house. What was that sound? A scream? The girl was screaming? He would sit a spell and observe the situation. Could it be that the preacher man was a man given to violence? Would he hit a woman? Maybe he wasn't the "man of God" he pretended to be. After all, he was a killer!

Dan whistled through his blackened teeth and settled himself in for a spell. He would bide his time and take in the situation.

Another scream pierced the silence and then an infant's cry bugled into the afternoon calm. *A baby?* The cries from the girl and the baby ceased and all was quiet once more. Dan formulated a plan in his evil, twisted mind. *I'll go into the cabin while the preacher is distracted and blow his head off before he knows what hit him. Without help that simpering girl and baby will die a slow death. It was perfect!*

Quickly he slipped down the embankment. Where was that dog gone to now? He appeared to be running off to chase after something in the distance. *Good.* He edged his way around the house and busted through the door. His rifle was ready.

Elaine Littau

The only occupants of the cabin were the girl and a newborn baby. Shoot, she hadn't even cleaned him up yet.

The girl's eyes were wide in horror but she appeared too weak to scream again. She grabbed the baby close to her and held on tight.

"Where's the preacher?" barked the man.

Nan opened her mouth but no sound escaped past her lips. Dan stood there in confusion. Now what? Fred wasn't there and it was useless to kill the girl. He might come get her later when she looked strong again, but he had no use for an ailing female. The babe made a small whimpering sound. Without hesitation he grabbed the baby from the little mother and tore the quilt off the bed and stuffed it around the helpless little creature. Dan stood for a brief moment and looked down at the starkly pale face. She had fainted and looked dead against the white sheet. The bed was covered in blood. *Poor, stupid kid, she just didn't have what it takes to make it in the wilderness.* He tucked the baby under his arm and ran. Fred wouldn't be very far away and he didn't want to be caught in the cabin with a dead girl.

He made good time scrambling up the embankment up to his mule. Old Brute was of a mind to run and that was fine with Dan. The hooves ate up many miles before he pulled him to a stop. While riding at break neck speed he had come up with a plan. The Utes were camped just a piece over that next rise. They were always buying slaves and kids. Maybe he could unload this baby for a good pile of pelts. He had thought that he would just knock him in the head and kill him, but if there was profit in it, he could put up with the crying a little longer. In fact the crying had stopped or at least gotten very strained. Maybe the kid would die before he got to the Injun camp.

Small trails of smoke stained the still, white sky as Dan rode in to the winter camp of the Utes. Women and children rose from the cooking fires and stared at him. The men boldly strode up to his mule.

"I have trade for you. We gather!"

The largest most aggressive man indicated with a nod to a nearby fire where three other more assuming men sat. "What is it, Boy Man?"

Dan's skin prickled over the stupid name they called him. He told them he was Dan and they enjoyed making sport of him.

"I found a newborn. His mother is dead. You will buy him from me." As he said this, he uncovered the baby. The baby was still covered in the bloody mess from his birth. When the cold air hit the little body, the baby howled a piercing wail. The men were startled and speechless.

"We may be able to take him from you. He would die if we didn't. You could give us five pelts."

"I could give YOU five pelts?"

"He is just one more mouth to feed to us. Make it ten pelts."

"You give me seven pelts and you can have this healthy man child."

A young man from the camp came near the screaming child and quietly spoke, "I will give you seven beaver pelts for this child."

The others looked at him and nodded their approval.

"Done." Dan waited next to the fire holding the crying baby while the young man fetched the seven choice beaver pelts. He wondered what in the world the Ute would do with the kid. *Probably make a sacrifice to a heathen god or something.* That made his skin crawl, but seven pelts was seven pelts.

"Seven pelts." The young man carefully transferred the newborn into his arms and walked to his teepee.

Dan observed the heathen, turned on his heel, and mounted Brute. There was no way he would spend the night here. The kid might die and he would have to give back the pelts. He gave a half-hearted salute to the man he supposed to be the chief and rode off.

Elaine Littau

Nan awoke to another strong pain in the back that spread across the front of her stomach. She cried out in pain. Over and over the spasms came. She pushed again and again as the pain wracked her body. When she felt she could push no longer another little baby boy was born. He struggled in the bed and gave forth a strong wail. Nan reached for him and put him to her breast. He ate hungrily.

Fred noticed the tracks in front of the cabin the moment he approached. They were fresh. Would Nan leave the cabin so close to her time? Maybe she was getting a little exercise. She had a good month before the baby came. Elmer slid off the front of the saddle like an expert.

"Here, Elmer, take these pelts to the shed and I'll put the horse in the barn."

Elmer ran to the shed and disposed of the pelts. He then joined Fred in the barn and helped him remove the saddle and blanket. He took an old cloth and began wiping down the big horse. Fred measured out some oats and filled the manger with sweet smelling hay. Fred rubbed his big hand through the little fellow's hair and mussed it up playfully. "Hey, Elmer, I'm gonna have to rename you Mop iffen we don't get some scissors to that head of hair of yours."

Elmer's smile looked just like warm rays of sunshine. The sparkling blue eyes were clear and free from pain and his mop of white/blonde hair was long and shiny. Elmer could grin like no other human he had ever known. "Come on, Kid, lets see what Nan has for us to eat."

The cabin was almost dark. The fire was the only light in the place. Fred swung his gaze around the room looking for Nan. He had decided that she was still out for a walk when he saw her face. "Oh, God! Help her!" He grabbed her hand. It was cool but not the icy cold that death settled into a body. She was very close to death. She was so pale. "Nan! Nan!" He lit a lamp and started from the blood that was staining the bed.

Elmer screamed, "Nan!"

Her eyes fluttered open briefly and closed just as quickly. Fred looked at her and saw the infant at her breast.

Nan's eyes flew open. Fred was not prepared for the stark terror that radiated from her eyes. "He took my baby!" she croaked.

"Who took your baby, Nan? The baby is right here!"

She breathed one quiet word, "Trap...per."

"Trapper? Nan! Nan! Look, the little baby is here! The trapper didn't take it." Fred tried to reason with Nan but she was holding on to life by a thread.

"Elmer, get a quilt out of the trunk on the other side of the room and bring it to me."

"Is Nan dead?"

"No, but we got to take care of her."

"Look at the baby! Is it all right? Is it a boy or a girl?"

"Elmer, just get the quilt and we will take care of Nan first."

Fred picked up the small little one and wrapped him in a soft blanket that Nan had made. He placed him in the newly made cradle next to the bed. "You are a little guy aren't you, boy? Elmer, it's a boy!"

Elmer brought the quilt to Fred and Fred asked him to put another log on the fire to heat up the stew that was on the fire hook.

"Elmer, I need you to watch that stew so that it doesn't burn and I need to doctor your sister. Please stay over there while I take care of her. If she wakes up, I'll holler at you and you can talk to her."

"Okay, Fred." Silently the tears streamed down his little face. He would be brave and not cry like a baby. He would try to pray for his beloved sister.

Fred was very concerned that Nan had already given birth to the baby. They were going to go his Mom and Dad's house this week so that Nan would have a doctor for delivery. Had he calculated wrong? No, it had been seven and a half months since the attack. The baby came early. He carefully bathed her frail, little body with a warm soapy rag. Maybe she would awaken and tell him more. She did not stir. The birth must have gone roughly because there was a lot of tearing on her body. He bound her up carefully. She had lost a lot of blood. The baby wasn't very big by coming so early, but Nan was a tiny woman. He put a fresh flannel gown on her and she moaned painfully.

Why did she think that the trapper took her baby? What was he to do to help her? He hated the thought of that trapper taking the helpless infant. "Lord, what can I do? She is so weak. Let her know that the baby is here next to her."

"Pray," was the answer.

"Please help her! Don't let her die! I love her so much!"

Blue Bird sat quietly stirring the venison stew inside her cozy home. Tears escaped her guarded eyes. She must keep working and not think of the sadness in her life. Just as she wiped the tears away the flap of the teepee opened and in came Strong Bear carrying a strange wrapping. "I have purchased something for you, my wife."

As he spoke he unwound the wrapping. She blinked in disbelief as she laid her eyes on the most beautiful sight her eyes could behold. It was a newborn baby boy! As the little one cried, Blue Bird asked, "Where did you get him, Bear?"

"A man found him. The mother is dead. The young one needs a mother. You need a son." Blue Bird became aware of the warm milk dripping down onto her stomach. The cries of the child brought the milk in as if it had been her own son crying. She put the baby to her breast and he sucked hungrily. Not too many days ago she buried her third child. She was a mother and yet not a mother. There would be no laughter of children in her home, until now. She had prayed for a son and one had been born to her. He had lived only three days. Now the Great God of the white man had given her another son. Tears flowed down her brown cheeks and she did nothing to hide them.

Chapter Twenty

Seven days passed since the birth of Nan's child. Fred could not understand why Nan insisted that one of the trappers had stolen her baby when little Teddy was in her arms. Tears streamed down her cheeks as she desperately tried to get Fred to understand. "The trapper came and took my baby! He did!"

"Nan, what are you saying? Do you not see little Teddy there in your arms?"

"Yes, but there was another baby!"

"Try to get some rest. We are heading to Mama and Papa's tomorrow. I will get you to the Doctor and he can help you get well."

"But the trapper came…"

"Nan, listen to me. You are safe. Elmer is safe and the baby is safe. The trapper is not here. Go to sleep."

Nan turned on her side and put little Teddy in the crook of her arm. He looked perfect to her. He had a head of soft, downy blonde hair. Maybe Fred was right. There was no trapper. Maybe she had dreamed of the horrible man coming and taking her baby. It seemed so real. First the birth of the child and then that awful leering face. Fred was right the trapper hadn't been here. It had been a bad dream during a difficult labor. Finally, she drifted off to the first peaceful sleep since the birth of her children.

Fred cleared the table and started packing the bedrolls for the trip to his parents. They would take most of the supplies they had left. The snow was thawing and the stars were out so it looked to him that the weather would be clear on the way down the pass. He packed most of their belongings because he had no plans of returning here to live. Nan's fear of the trapper was a tangible thing. He wouldn't have her living in fear. He

Elaine Littau

looked at her face and noted the peaceful look that it held. He hadn't seen that in quite some time. Little Teddy was wiggling around so Fred retrieved him from his place next to Nan and held him to his chest.

"You are quite the little man! Look at you. You are so little, yet you think you should be going somewhere. Well, you get to meet your grandma and grandpa in a couple of days. How about that?"

Elmer came into the cabin after watering the stock. He edged closer to Fred and Teddy. "You want to hold him, Elmer?"

"Nope. Not yet. My fingers are like ice. I best warm them up first lest he let out a yell to wake the dead."

"Good thinking, Pard. What do you think of your little nephew?"

"He is so little; I hope nothing bad happens to him. Do you think he will be alright?"

"He has already fattened up some this past week so I think he will be okay, but we will let doc take a look at him to be sure."

"How will we keep him warm on the way to grandpa's house?"

"Lookie here, I traded the traps and chickens for a cradle board at the Indian camp yesterday. I knew that the people in James' camp could use them. James was gone so I gave them to a man called Strong Bear. His squaw showed me how to wrap him up and tie him in just right. I think he will do well."

"There is fur and deer skin and all kinds of beads and stuff. It is kinda pretty, too." Elmer thought it would be a great way for his little nephew to travel in the cold weather.

"Pard, I didn't forget about you. See here, I got you some new deer skin trousers and moccasins."

Elmer tried them on. The trousers tucked inside the moccasins, which laced all the way up to his knees. Man, did they feel good compared to the boots he had been wearing. He had tried not to let on that he had outgrown them weeks ago.

"You have been growing like a weed ever since you had your teeth taken care of. Those old boots were about to lose hold of those big toes of yours and your pants were almost half way to your knees!"

Elmer grinned at the exaggeration. The trousers were a few inches up his leg but not that far.

"I also got you this traveling coat from the trading post." Elmer was in awe. He had never seen anything as colorful and warm looking as this new coat. It was a creamy color with wide stripes of red and yellow across the chest. It looked like it was made of an Indian blanket. He put it on and boy was it warm! He had never owned anything so luxurious!

"Thank you so much Fred! I love it!" Then Elmer looked anxiously toward the small figure in the bed. "How will we keep Nan warm enough? She needs this coat more than I do."

"No, Elmer, I got something special for her. While I was in the Indian camp I asked the squaw that I traded goods with for her advice as to how to move a very sick person down the pass and keep them warm. I explained that a travois would be far too rough and bumpy down the trail. She agreed and showed me how to wrap and bundle Nan up in blankets and a buffalo robe somewhat like the cradleboard. Nan will have to ride in front of me on the horse while I hold her like an infant. You will have to let me strap little Teddy on your back. You must listen for his cries and care for him."

Elmer's eyes were very serious as Fred explained the traveling arrangements. The pack mule would follow Fred's horse and Elmer would be in front of Fred on the other mule so that Fred could keep his eye on Elmer and baby Teddy. If Nan would have been getting stronger, the trip could have waited a couple of months, but she seemed to be withering before his eyes. He knew he could not chance the loss.

Elaine Littau

Bright and early the next morning Fred packed the items on the Ruby. He got Sonny ready. No saddle, just saddle blankets. He saddled Moon Shadow for Elmer. The bedrolls were in place and grub for the trip in the saddlebags. He spread the little furs on the bed and then the soft blankets on top. He placed Teddy in the middle and tightly wrapped them around him swaddling him with arms wrapped tightly to his side. He placed the infant thus wrapped, in the cradleboard and began tying the laces snuggly. He placed the soft deerskin over the head frame and made a cozy little tent over the little face. Elmer stood beside the bed and allowed Fred to place the small burden on his back.

Fred threw the big buffalo hide on the bed and placed deerskin and quilts on top. He lifted Nan from the rocker. She had been dressed in a long deer skin dress and moccasins like Elmer's. He placed her in the middle of the covers. He began to wrap the quilt, deerskin and buffalo hide tightly around her from head to toe. He then took strips of deer hide and tied them around her snuggly. Nan meekly lay there feeling the warmth of the nest he made for her. How lovingly he smoothed the covers. He was as tender in his care of her as he had been with baby Teddy. He wrapped a heavy scarf over her head and left her a peephole so that she could see. He placed Elmer and his little bundle on Moon Shadow and came into the cabin to get Nan. He carried her to Sonny and sat her sideways on top of him. Fred then climbed on him and put his arms around Nan and held the reins. Ruby trailed behind them with packs on her back. "Nan, I am going to move you closer to me so that you can lean back and I will hold you in my arms. We will move slowly so that you will not be jolted. Try to rest as much as you can. Sleep if at all possible. Let me know when you need to stop to rest."

Nan nodded and nestled in his arms. She had no fear when Fred was this close to her. His strong arms seemed to hold her effortlessly and she did sleep. When she woke the sun was high in the clear blue sky. She saw the tops of the lovely spruce trees and the white bark tops of the aspen. She turned her head ever so slightly and saw the handsome, sun-darkened face of her husband. She observed the lines around his eyes as he squinted in the bright daylight. As he glanced down at her, she was struck, yet again, at the bright color of blue that twinkled in his large eyes. He smiled at her and gave her a wink. "You doing alright, little Misses?"

"I feel like a baby being rocked in my mama's arms."

"Good. It shouldn't take but a couple of days to get down to town. We will stop in a bit to eat some of the cold biscuits and bacon I packed. You can stretch your legs if you want, or lay down flat. We won't take a long break but we will make camp about an hour before dark. Of course, Teddy will let us know when he is in need of nursing."

In another hour they stopped for dinner. Fred placed blankets on a grassy spot that the snow had melted from. He unwrapped Nan and brought Teddy to her. She laughed as she removed the deerskin tent from the cradleboard. Teddy was sucking his bottom lip in hunger. When he saw his mother he began to whimper. "Come, little one. Mama has your dinner ready for you."

Fred took little Teddy out of the cradleboard and placed him in Nan's arms. He ate hungrily and fell fast asleep. Fred rearranged the covers and laced him back into his little cocoon.

"He looks very content doesn't he?"

"So, Nan, are you content? How are you really doing?"

"If you are asking about my seeing the trapper, I have decided that maybe it was a horrible dream or something while I was in labor. I don't really know how to explain something that seemed so real to me."

"You will feel better as soon as we can get your strength back. Ma will see to that!"

"Yep, your Mama is a nurturer that's for sure."

"Elmer, you doing okay? How's the coat working?"

"Warm as toast!"

"Was Teddy too heavy for you?"

"He don't weigh nothing."

"Well then, let's get moving."

The air grew warmer the farther down the pass they traveled. Nan could hear the streams crashing down the mountainside. They sounded alive. Birds sang in the sunshine and she could hear the sound of the hooves on rocks and dirt. She asked Fred, "Is the snow all gone where we are now?"

"Let me set you up a little straighter so that you can see more."

He shifted her into an upright position and she could see the lay of the land. Down the pass most of the snow was melted. There were very few patches left here and there. Wild flowers were springing forth in a riot of color across the big meadow. She could see that they were almost down the mountain. It would grow dark soon, so they had to make camp. They would be in town within a week if they got an early start. If she knew anything about Fred, it was that they always got an early start. That thought brought a smile to her lips. Fred looked down at her and saw the smile, and prayed that he would be able to make her smile like that all the time.

Fred and Elmer set up camp together. Nan held little Teddy in the cradleboard until the spot where she would sleep was made ready. She was given orders to lean against the pile of saddle blankets until her bed ready. She was not allowed to stand with the baby or even walk by herself. She did not resist the orders because she really was too tired to fight them. Fred lifted her and the baby into his arms and carried her to a bed made of the buffalo hide that had been wrapped around her all day, as well as the deer skins and quilts. He added another buffalo hide to cover her with. Fred explained that he and Elmer would be sharing the bed with her and the baby eventually. Their body heat would keep all of them warm. Elmer unlaced baby Teddy from his trappings and laid him next to Nan. Elmer gave both of them a quick kiss on the forehead and ran to find firewood. Presently he returned with his arms full of dead branches.

"Great job, Pard. Tear the small twigs off, then the larger ones and then break the biggest ones across your knee like this." Fred demonstrated.

Fred drug a large dead log to the camp and began chopping it with his axe. He split it and split it again. Before long Elmer and Fred had a nice fire going and Nan watched from the vantage point of her warm bed. Teddy was sleeping soundly after nursing. Nan snuggled closer to the little one. He was so soft and smelled so sweet. She couldn't breathe in enough of him. The little lips smacked and made sucking noises. His soft dark lashes swept across the rosy cheeks. He was growing and filling out. She watched his little chest rise and fall in deep sleep. She was so glad she had him. She was glad he hadn't been stolen as she had at first thought. It had been so real…but it wasn't real. Her baby was here next to her sleeping like an angel.

After an early start the four travelers arrived at Ma and Pa's home in the early afternoon of the eighth day. It had taken a little longer than Fred had estimated due to the baby needing nourishment every few hours. It had been a long time since he had to factor in the needs of an infant, but Fred didn't mind.

"Bless my soul, its Fred and Nan…and Elmer too of course!"

"And baby Teddy!" Elmer added.

"Baby Teddy! You mean that you have already had that child!"

Elmer turned around so that Grandma could see the infant in the cradleboard. "Dear me, he is so tiny! Honey, he is too small! Is he okay?"

"As far as we can tell he is fine, Ma," Fred said.

"Get him out of that contraption so that I can hold my grandson! And, Nan, where is Nan?"

"Right here!" Nan cried.

"Lands sakes, girl, you looked like a sack of feed or something!"

Nan laughed and said, "I kinda feel like a sack of feed or something!"

Elaine Littau

Pa came running out of the house and observed Nan in her confining position. "You want me to set you free, sweetie?"

"Please do!"

"Nan, just stand there and don't try to walk. I will carry you." Fred said.

"Why, what's wrong that she can't walk herself?" Pa asked.

"She is too weak to go more that a step without falling."

"I'm sorry I'm such a baby!"

"Nonsense, lets just get all of you inside."

Fred lifted Nan and carried her inside followed by his Ma and Pa with Elmer and Teddy.

"She will need to take to the bed right now, if you don't mind, Ma."

"Bring her to your old room, son." Martha quickly turned down the covers with one hand and she held little Teddy with the other. Fred laid her gently on the bed and told her to rest while he got her things unloaded. He would help her into a clean nightgown as soon as he brought everything in. She nodded and found that the soft feather bed was lulling her to sleep against her efforts to stay awake.

As Fred exited the room he found his father in the kitchen. "Pa, can you please get the doc for me to look at Nan and Teddy? I think Teddy is all right, although he is terribly small, but Nan isn't getting her strength back at all."

The kindly doctor listened attentively to Fred as he described the day of Teddy's birth.

"Now, I have a suspicion that there is more to the story than what you have told me, Fred."

"Doc, she has been confused and frightened every since that day."

"In what way?"

"She...ah...thought that someone came into the cabin and stole the baby."

"Who would do that? Where would an idea like that come from?"

"She had seen some trappers that she was afraid of. They are very rough living men, you know, so…"

"She thought one of them came to the cabin?"

"Actually, she thought that one of them stole her baby to be exact. I had to reassure her that baby Teddy was there and had not been stolen."

"That doesn't make sense. Why would a trapper want a baby? You let her hold little Teddy and see him right away?"

"Yes. I think that she finally has realized that she has had a very terrible dream. She has finally begun to eat a little more."

"She is very thin, Fred. We will have to watch her very carefully. Let me examine her more closely and you stay here."

Nan opened her tired eyes as the doctor came into the room.

"May I examine you to be certain that you are healing properly from the birth of that little boy of yours?"

"Yes, doctor."

Dr. Benson was amazed at exactly how thin Nan had become. He had not realized how bony she was until he pressed on her stomach.

"Little Mama, you are going to have to eat! Teddy needs his mother to be strong and healthy. I want you to drink plenty of milk and force yourself to eat a plate of food each meal time."

"I will try."

The doctor lowered his voice, "Nan, why are you so fearful? Tell me what is so heavy on your mind."

Nan began sobbing great and terrible moaning sobs.

"What is it? Talk to me girl. I promise I won't tell anyone anything if you don't want me to."

"Oh, doctor, I don't know where to begin!"

"Start at the first time you began to feel fear and we will go from there."

Nan began by telling about escaping from her stepmother with Elmer. She told about the kidnap and rape by the trappers and ended with her fear that one of them had come into the cabin and stolen her baby.

Dr. Benson sat there listening to the frail girl tell her story. There was a lot of suffering for one so young to digest. "Nan, have you told anyone about any of this?"

"Fred knows everything...and Elmer."

"The baby was fathered by one of the trappers then..."

"Yes."

"Unless when you and Fred came together..."

"No, Fred has been very understanding and kind to me. He hasn't touched me."

"I see. No one else knows about the rape?"

"Fred wanted to protect me from vicious tongues."

"That was probably wise. Do his Ma and Pa know?"

"No."

"He is very protective of you."

"Yes."

"Do you blame him for not being around when the men attacked you?"

"No. I don't think so. Doctor, the dream I had about one of them stealing my baby was just so real, I don't know how to deal with it."

"In medical school we learned that the mind does play tricks on people who have been through great trauma. I think that may be the case here. But, young one, you are going to be fine. When you become frightened look at that little baby and realize that he is here and safe. Fred and Elmer are devoted to you and will always be here."

"Doctor, I have a very odd question to ask you, if I may."

"Yes?"

"Why? Why do so many things go wrong in my life?"

"Nan, we may never know the answer to that but my opinion is that you have already had your share of tragedy, so things will definitely be better from this point on."

"Promise?"

"If you try hard to take good care of yourself, yep, I promise."

As the doctor left the room he saw Fred standing in the kitchen. "Doctor, you were in there such a long time. Is Nan going to be all right? Is she…all right?"

"Fred will you walk with me?"

"Surely. Is she . .what's wrong with her? Will she live?"

The evening air was brisk as they strolled down the street toward the doctor's residence. "Yes, if she finds the will to live."

"What do you mean? Could she die?"

"Nan has been through a lot. It is a wonder that she has lived this long." Doc darted a look at Fred's face. Fred looked startled. The doctor stopped at the door of his office, "Fred, she told me everything. About the beatings from her stepmother and the attack of the trappers and the way you rescued her."

Fred pushed his hat back and wiped the sweat from his brow. "I can't believe that she told you all of that. I don't know what to say."

"Fred, I think you need to tell me about what you plan to do from here on."

"What do you mean?"

"The way I see it is that you married the girl from pity or guilt and now you don't know what to do."

"No. You have it all wrong! I love her. With all my heart I love her!"

Doc squinted his eyes and looked hard at Fred. "Tell me how that came about."

"At first I thought she was a lot younger than she is. The thought of love never entered my mind. When I came to the cabin and Nan had been taken, I thought I couldn't stand it if I never saw her again. I had to go after her."

"You married her because…"

"You know what happened to her. I thought that if she was in the family way I should stand by her…so no one could find fault in her. You know how people are!"

"Did she care for you?"

"I think she was relieved to be married because her step-parents couldn't get to her then."

"And now?"

"I think she loves me as a brother."

"Is that enough for you? Will you stay with her?"

"Yes. Even if she never loves me the way I love her I will stay with her. I also love Elmer and Teddy."

"So Teddy is to be regarded as your son?"

"Of course. Doc, please don't let any of this get out. It would hurt Nan."

"I will tell no one."

"Doc, I have been feeling so guilty about loving Nan. I feel as if I am taking away from the love I had for Claire. Claire and Joy were everything to me. I have held them in my heart so long and never want to forget what we had together as a family."

"Fred, Claire and Joy have been gone for nigh unto two years now. She loved you so much. I don't think she would want you to make an idol of your love."

"What do you mean?"

"When you hold the memory someone that close to your heart and don't let anyone else in, you have made a shrine and set her memory up as something to worship. God is the only one we are to worship."

"I never saw it that way. I just have been missing them so much."

"I think God gave Nan and Elmer to you just in the nick of time. You were away from everyone for such a long time."

"I'm glad that they came when they did. I think Claire would approve of Nan. Nan is much different than Claire, but it is like comparing sunset and sunrise. They each have a beauty of spirit."

"Spoken like a man in love."

"Thank you for your insight, friend."

"I think Nan needs to know that you love her not as a sister, but as a woman. You need to tell her so that she will try harder to get well."

"You don't think it would confuse her more?"

"Trust me, Fred, you must tell her today."

Fred eased the door to the bedroom open and gazed at Nan nursing the infant. She was stretched out on the bed with the child nestled by her side. It was a beautiful picture. She looked up at him and smiling said, "Teddy is nursing better now. I think he looks better don't you?"

"Yes, you both look much better since you arrived here. Nan, I need to tell you something before I lose my nerve."

Nan paled and put her hand to her throat in despair.

"No, Nan, you aren't in danger. I just need to tell you that… well…you mean everything to me. I love you. I don't expect anything from you but I do hope that with time we can be more than friends. You might grow to love me like a husband. If you do, I would be so happy. If you don't, I won't be changing the way I feel about you. There, I said it. It needed to be said."

"Fred, I am afraid that you think you love me and what you really feel is pity. You don't have to worry about loving me that way. I know that you have a good heart."

"I may have felt enormous pity for you and Elmer at first. Goodness knows I have! Let me tell you this, if you were no longer in my life I feel like I would die. I know what love feels like. I do love you. I felt guilty because I love you so much… mainly because I felt I was being untrue to Claire—but Nan, you have captured a brand new place in my heart. The heart that I thought had died two years ago. It beats for you."

"Oh Fred!" A bright smile chased across her tired face and tears stood in her eyes, "I do love you!"

Fred knelt next to the bed and gathered her and Teddy into his arms, "We are truly a family now!"

Elaine Littau

Chapter Twenty-One

Mary threw out the last of the wash water onto the large garden. It was the last of the diapers washed and up on the line. Her sweet baby boy lay in a basket next to the clothesline. She breathed in the smell of the drying clothes flapping in the breeze. The lye soap and sunshine concocted a fragrance that could not be duplicated. Funny, the smell took her right back to her childhood. Her Ma had her help with hanging up the wash. She enjoyed the chore. It was one chore complemented by her Ma. *Goodness, there surely was a lot to wash on wash-day.* She stood back and surveyed the clothes on the line. She almost giggled when she saw Mr. Dewey's overalls flapping in the wind. They almost looked to be walking. There were dozens of diapers all lined up crisp and clean. She was right proud of her expertise in the laundry department. Her Ma always told her that you could tell a woman who was worth her salt by the cleanliness of her laundry. It had to be done on Monday, rain or shine. It was a mark of a lazy woman if it were put off to Tuesday. Tuesday had its own set of chores. *Man alive, I have wasted way too much time thinking on the past this morning. I have much to do!*

She tested the corner of one of the diapers and found that it was almost dry already. She would feed her little darling first and then gather them in to fold up. Feeding him was her favorite activity ever. She had the luxury of rocking him and trying to memorize every part of his little face. She observed his long lashes that softly brushed against his cheeks while he slept. Those eyes! Blue and sharp, they looked intelligently and lovingly at her. She could gaze into those eyes forever. His little mouth looked like a baby rosebud. He was perfect.

Mr. Dewey was even fond of him. He had gone to Trinidad to see the lawyer this week to "set some of the estate to rights." It was good to have him gone for the week so that she could cuddle and kiss her sweet baby. Mr. Dewey didn't want her "fussing" over him very much, but Mary had so much love bustin' in her heart that she couldn't help but kiss the soft rosy cheeks. Baby Sammy cooed and smacked his rosebud lips. "Li'l Darlin,' let me put you in your cradle while I gather those diapers."

She laid the infant in the cradle next to the kitchen table and brought in a basket full of diapers and a few shirts. She laid the shirts across the back of the chair and began folding the snowy white diapers. Sammy watched as she flipped them and snapped them efficiently in the air and then smoothed them into perfect triangles and stacked them on the big wooden table.

As she folded and smoothed, she looked at the expressive little eyes and though, *"I love him so much. Will old Sam teach him to be cruel and mean? Somehow, I must teach him to be kind. Kind? Me teach him to be kind?"* Tears gathered in the corners of her faded blue eyes and she tried to piece together a plan. This might be more difficult than being accepted into the town. *I have been playing a part for Mr. Dewey and the women of the town, but I have to be in earnest with this innocent little one. I want him to trust me…and I want to be able to trust him too when he grows up.* She sat there in serious reflection until a knock to the door started her out of her thoughts.

"Mrs. Dewey, Mary, are you there?"

Mary jumped up and opened the door to the voice of her new pastor. "Yes, Parson, please do come in. You will have to pardon the mess, but I have been doing my Monday chores. Do come into the parlor and I will bring you a glass of cool water."

"That's alright, Mary, I just came by to see the little fellow and to remind you that we are having special services tonight. I want you to be there with Mr. Dewey at seven o'clock."

"Parson, Mr. Dewey is out of town this week."

"Fine, but be sure that you attend tonight."

"Is it a business meeting or missions meeting?"

"No, there is a man who is very special to me coming to speak to our congregation. I want the church house to be full for him. He hasn't preached for several years and I want him to be encouraged with a good crowd."

"I see, well…"

"I won't take no for an answer. I must be going. Good day."

"Good day, Parson."

Mary sank into her chair and stormed inside, *"That is just like a man, tellin' a body what to do! Course, I'll go! I don't want Mrs. Waide talkin' behind my back and I don't want the new pastor's wife to get the wrong idea about me."*

She selected one of her newer dresses that she hadn't worn much. She was saving it to wear to the next sewing circle, but if this meeting were so all-fired important, she would wear it. She laid out a fresh little smock for Sammy and packed a few diapers into a clean flour sack. She would bath him and herself and make a good impression on them all. *Why couldn't a body just be themselves and be accepted? I'm so tired of playing these stupid games. It was so much easier when I didn't care, but I want the best for my son so the act must continue. I'll smile all evening if it breaks my face off! They won't know what I am thinking behind the smile. That will make it easier. I do find myself laughing at how gullible they are and all. Maybe it won't be so hard.* With that, Mary began preparing for the special church service.

Chapter Twenty-Two

Fred was sweating profusely as he unloaded the boxcar for his father. The little store was busy these days and shipments came more frequently. He had asked Pa if he could work for him while he, Nan, and Elmer lived at the old home. Pa had told him that he would be glad to pay him so that they could get into a little house of their own. He straightened his back into a stretch to get a kink out of it when he spotted a face from his past.

Stepping off the train and onto the platform was a man dressed in his Sunday best black suit. He donned a black hat and would have been mistaken for a riverboat gambler if it had not been for the worn black Bible he held comfortably in his left hand. He carried it as if it were a glove that he wore. There was no thought of it as he made his way through the press of passengers departing the train. His easy gait distinguished him from the rest of the weary travelers. Fred grinned in spite of the catch in his back.

"Hey there, Parson! What brings you to these parts?"

The handsome face turned toward the friendly greeting, "I'll be, if it isn't the Prophet! What are *you* doing here?"

Fred flushed at the reference to his old nickname from Bible school. "I live here now. You tell me your tale now."

"I came here from Denver on my way to Campo."

"Marcus, are you here long enough to eat some dinner with me?"

"Sure, my stage doesn't leave until tomorrow morning."

"Then you must eat supper with us."

"Us?"

"Yes, my parents, wife, son, and brother-in-law"

"I wouldn't be imposing?"

"Never! Ma loves to see friends of mine."

Elaine Littau

"I would be much obliged. I will secure a room at the hotel and we can catch up on old times. I have much to tell you and many questions for you also."

"Let me help you with your gear and we will get that room taken care of."

The hotel clerk peered over his spectacles at the two handsome yet distinctly different young men. One was the familiar face of the hard working Young boy. The other was a stranger to Trinidad and appeared to be an intellectual sort. He had strong features and honest brown eyes, yet the calluses on his hands had softened up some. "How can I be of service, Fred?"

"George, this is my best friend from Bible school, Marcus Hall. He is a true man of God. If you rent him a room, you will be compelled to come to church every time the door is opened, just because you came near to this man."

"I don't know that I like that so much, Fred. I kinda like my old fishin' hole on quiet Sunday mornings," the good-natured clerk whined.

Marcus grinned at the old man, "We'll have to have a nice long talk after I catch up with Fred. You might be apt to change your mind."

"Here's your key. It's the room clean across the building from me. Make sure you don't come to visit me in room 212 tonight at ten o'clock. I won't have coffee made and a list of questions that I have been wondering about for years. Nope, you just let me live my life and you live yours."

"I'll make sure to keep that in mind, George."

Fred and Marcus made their way to the tiny hotel room and left off the trunk and valise from the train. Marcus opened the window for some fresh air. "I normally would think that it was George that God directed me to town to see, but I do know that I must talk with you also."

Fred felt a nervous jerk in his chest. He didn't really want to open up his soul to this righteous man. "I have been working

on ole George for a long time. I know he really needs God..."
his voice trailed off.

"My friend, I knew that you were in this town. The Lord
placed you on my heart and I haven't been able to shake it.
Please tell me about yourself."

"You know most everything about me, Marcus."

"No, I do know that you were a fine minister in one of
these small towns. Something happened that hurt you and
you took your wife and daughter up to the top of a mountain—somewhere by Silverton. I also know that they died of
influenza and you stayed there grieving."

"Like I said, you already know everything!" Fred didn't
mean to raise his voice as much as he did.

Marcus sat down on the bed leaving the one straight-
backed chair for Fred. "Sit. You and I have much to talk
about."

Fred quietly sat on the chair. His body was suddenly
weary. His soul was desolate and he didn't want to open up
old wounds.

"Tell me what happened at your little church."

"They just told me to leave. You know the way it goes.
Some of the elders ask you to leave so that someone more to
their liking can come to pastor them. It was just a matter of
business."

"I know better! There was a reason that we named you the
Prophet. You had zeal that put Elijah to shame!"

"I was young then."

"You are young now! And that was your first pastorate!
Don't try to get out of answering me. I heard that it had something to do with Indians and prostitutes?"

"If you must know, I was going to the alleys where the poor
fellows drank themselves into a stupor. I helped them by feeding them and letting them sleep in the barn next to the parsonage. When they were sober I prayed with them and they came
to the Lord. Some of them went right back to drinking and I
would find them in the alley again and again. I kept bringing

them home and some of them got gloriously saved. I mean it! They came to church every Sunday. One of them was in love with a prostitute named Abby. He brought her to church one Sunday morning and she came to the front to accept Jesus as her Savior. The look on her face changed from dark to daylight. It was an amazing change. I was so excited that I didn't notice that some of the people of the church left the meeting before dismissal. Abby went home and told the other girls about the change in her life. She had nowhere to go, so she had to stay at the brothel. The man who loved her married her the next day. One by one prostitutes came to the church and found God. The owner of the brothel was angry. I expected that. What I didn't expect was the anger of the church folks. They didn't want former prostitutes in their church."

Marcus gave a knowing nod, "'The people of God' are some of the most callous folks around, that's for sure."

"They were also enraged about the young Indian families that started attending after I prayed with them at their camp. They said that they were afraid for their lives."

"What happened then?"

"They called me in to a special meeting with the elders. The jist of the meeting was that there were getting to be more 'dirty sinners' saved and attending than 'decent people' who had founded the church. They told me to start a mission church for the riff raff on Sunday afternoons and let their tidy congregation attend with like-minded people."

"Did you do it?"

"No! I told them that they were to be the godly examples as identified in I Timothy. They were to nurture these new babies in Christ. They said that if I would not do as they asked that I must leave the church and take 'those people' with me."

"How did that play out?"

"The next day was Sunday and I wanted to address the congregation to tell them I was moving on. The church was packed with most of the town's people, most of which had not come to Christ yet. I stood at the pulpit and spoke on the

Great Commission. I told them that I was not going to be their pastor anymore and that God would send them someone soon.

People began to cry. Some who were not schooled in church decorum, shouted out, 'No!' I reassured them all that God loved them and that Claire and I loved them too."

There was a long period of silence as the two sat in the tiny hotel room. Fred's cracking voice broke the silence, "One of the elders stood and informed the crowd that a new mission would be established for all the new converts to attend on Sunday afternoons. Sinners are not stupid, Marcus, they are just away from God. One of the store clerks, a new convert, stood and asked me, 'Fred, are you going to be preaching at the new mission?'

I had to answer him and I hated to answer him. The sentence was forming on my mind when one of the 'decent' church ladies stood up and declared that if it hadn't been for the 'Injuns and riff raff' the little church would be doing just fine. The church was stifling as most of the new converts stood and quietly filed out of the church. I have to tell you my heart broke then and there. I looked at Claire and she looked like death herself."

"Did they start a mission church?"

"No."

"While Claire and I were packing to move to the mountain, I went to each new convert and tried to pray with them. Some of them allowed me to pray, but most of them were so hurt by the 'good church people,' they didn't want anything to do with their God either. I couldn't blame them. I was angry at God too."

"So you moved to a mountain. Did you find healing there?"

"Claire was very despondent. I guess I was too. Our little girl was our only joy at that time. We had become cynical and disheartened. We were so hurt. We hadn't been there long before they came down with influenza. I nursed them as best

Elaine Littau

as I could. They didn't last a day. I laid next to them waiting to die with them. I never got sick. I prayed for death! How I prayed for death! When I dug their graves, I dug mine too. I knew that God would answer this prayer. I laid them in the ground and covered them up. Then I lay down in the bottom of my grave too.

"I must have slept for a couple of days in there. I heard someone calling my name. It was one of the Indians who was a new convert. James carried me to his camp and cared for me as if I were a newborn. I grew stronger, yet the grief was more than I can explain. I convinced them to let me go back to the cabin.

"After a few nights alone, I decided to go to Silverton. I shook God off like an old blanket as I went into the saloon. I saw a few familiar faces sitting at the tables. Some of them were the drunkards who I had fed, and some of them were prostitutes that Claire and I had taken in. They all looked down and headed for the door. I yelled for some whiskey. I cursed God. I pronounced to the whole group that I was through with religion and all of its trappings. I told them I had nothing to live for and that my family was dead and God was too as far as I was concerned.

"One of the girls that Claire had reached out to, Betsy, came over to me and put her head on my shoulder. It made me think of Claire. I drank and got good and drunk. I let her take me to her room. I stayed with her for days. I paid her gold for her love. When I went back to the cabin I was as low as a man can get. Whenever the memories became too hard for me, I went to Silverton and to Betsy. Every time I came back to the cabin I heard God's voice telling me to come to Him and He would give me rest, but I didn't want Him anymore."

"Is your new wife the…a…girl from Silverton?"

"Nan? No. That is a story in and of itself. I was planning to go away, far from my Mother and Father and anyone else who had ever heard of me. I was tired of the saloon patrons calling me 'preacher' when I was living so far from God. I wanted to lose myself in the wilderness and never come back to civilization, when my Pa came up the mountain with this little girl and her brother who were in terrible need."

"Little girl?"

"She looked a bunch younger than she was."

"How did you come to marry her?"

"When I found out that she was sixteen years old and had been living up on the mountain with me for months, I decided that marrying her was the only decent thing I could do to save her reputation. I didn't want any of those religious gooses to have anything bad to say about an innocent girl."

"Did you love her?"

"Not at first, but she has my heart now and she loves me too."

"You are not living on the mountain anymore?"

"No, since our child was born, I wanted him to be close to doctors if the need arises. I also wanted to let Ma and Pa get to know him. I realize that they suffered loss at the death of Claire and Joy too…"

"It will be good to meet your new family."

"They are probably wondering what has become of me by now. Let's go."

Fred was nervous. "Pa, I don't think I will be able to go through with this tonight! "

"Just keep putting one foot in front of the other, boy."

"Walking isn't my problem. Talking to these people is."

"Fred, you won't be talking to them. You will be preaching to them. There is a difference."

"How did I let Marcus Hall talk me into this?"

"As I recall, it wasn't exactly Pastor Hall that worked on you so much as it was the Lord."

"Pa, I haven't preached since before Claire and Joy died! How can I just up and preach now?"

"So, don't do it then."

"What?" Fred cried.

"Don't preach tonight."

"I have to preach tonight!"

"Why?"

"God has given me a message for these people."

"Talk to me, son. Tell me how you know that you have a message for this particular group of people."

"Let me see...How did it begin? I was praying one morning and reading the Bible when a Scripture passage just burned into my soul as I was reading it. I thought it was meant for Nan and was going to go show it to her when the Lord impressed me to be still. It was burning inside me so hot that I felt I must share it with Nan. It was a Scripture meant for her. I knew it! But...I knew that I was not to share it with her at that time. I began praying and asking God to show me why He was giving me all these things to say and why He was making this particular passage so alive to me. I read it again and knew that first, it was for me; and then it was for others. *Who?* I asked. I didn't get an answer for days."

"Is that when you saw Mark Hall?" Nate asked.

"Yes, I was helping unload one of the boxcars of supplies for the store and I saw Mark. I was surprised to see him. I hadn't seen him since we were at Seminary together. He was startled when I called him by name. We embraced and swapped stories. He said that God sent him to talk with me. He asked me if I would come down to Campo and preach at his church. He wouldn't take no for an answer."

"Let's look at your tie. Is it straight?" Nate fumbled with the string tie.

"It is as good as it's gonna get."

Fred entered the small kitchen. Nan was sitting in the cozy room rocking the baby as Martha was describing the nuances of cooking the perfect angel food cake. Nan had a contented smile tugging at the corner of her lovely mouth. She looked relaxed and happy. Health had come to her and she looked like a young school maid. Today she had chosen to braid her shiny black hair. Each braid was held together with a blue ribbon. Wisps of curls that had escaped the braids framed the pretty face. "Love, are you going to be alright while I go down to Campo? Are you sure you don't want to come with me?"

A small shadow crossed Nan's brow briefly as she contemplated going to the town from which she and Elmer had escaped so long ago. "No, dear one, I will stay here and keep your Ma company." The truth be told, Nan was still struggling with going back to the old hometown with all of the memories attached to it. She was unsure of what she would say or do for that matter if she ran on to Mr. or Mrs. Dewey. She knew that as a married woman, they had no hold on her. She was not sure about Elmer. She was not willing to risk letting him fall into their hands.

Fred crossed the room and planted a small kiss on baby Teddy's forehead. Nan smelled the fresh scent of shaving soap as Fred hovered close to the babe. He turned his merry, lightening blue eyes onto his pretty wife and exchanged a bright smile. Did she know that his heart was bursting with joy? The kiss she placed on his cheek answered him in the affirmative. "Come home as soon as you can, Fred," she said.

"I will. When I return we can start moving into the cottage down the lane if you are up to it." He grinned.

"Your ma and I have been cleaning and preparing the house for days. We will be ready when you get home."

Fred grabbed his mother and gave her a bear hug. "Pray, little woman, pray. I am counting on you to hold me up to the Lord for His help while I preach."

"Your Pa and I will be in constant prayer for you while you are gone."

"Nan, I need your prayers too."

"I will do my best," she said.

"So long, I will be back soon."

Elaine Littau

Fred climbed onto the train as it was leaving the station. He had to run the half mile from his folk's house. He allowed that he spent a little too long in his goodbyes. He felt a grin creep upon his face. He was a happy man. With that thought he reached into his bag and retrieved his worn Bible and began to read. After reading, dozing and taking his lunch, Fred began to observe the beauty of the scenery passing by his window. The sun was stealing over the mountains and site seeing was almost over for the day. The sky was spread with a golden glow. Darkness fell quickly. The stars emerged one by one like reluctant parishioners entering a church. The light cloud cover kept most of the heavenly bodies hidden from view. Thoughts began to step into Fred's mind slowly and surely. *"Am I ready to preach again? Will I experience God's Presence as I did in bygone days? Is He still with me?"*

The thoughts marched through his head to the rhythm of the wheels of the train. Eventually Fred was sound asleep.

The conductor passed through the almost vacant car and spoke to the lone passenger. "Next stop, Campo."

Fred opened his eyes and nodded to the older gentleman. "Thank you, sir."

"Get ready for a quick exit. Campo is only a whistle stop. Good day, young man."

"God be with you."

Chapter Twenty-Three

Reverend Mark Hall stepped up to the pulpit and surveyed the crowd gathered for the special meeting. There was the usual group of Pharisees, he thought of the self-righteous group. There were the sweet-faced couples who came to truly worship God. There were people who were totally away from God who came for the social standing that church attendance secured in the community, and there were the people who were seeking something that could bring them peace. Quietly Mary Dewey entered the sanctuary with her new baby. Mark smiled and was glad that she had come. There had been times in prayer that the Lord had put her troubled face before him. When he first met her, he hadn't noticed the unsettled spirit in her, but since praying specifically for her he had seen a tortured soul behind those eyes. She held her own with the women of the church, but he knew that she was forcing herself to be someone unfamiliar to herself. The door opened once more and an elderly woman who had recently lost her dear husband came in to join the number. He smiled warmly at his new congregation. They had accepted his appointment to the church in stride. He had so recently come to them that they had yet to complete their opinion of him and his family. They knew only a portion of the fire of God that burned in his bones.

"Friends, I want to begin the service in a different way. I want to give Brother Fred Young as much time as possible to minister to you. I would like to begin with a song that an acquaintance of mine, R.E. Hudson, wrote. I would like for you to listen to the words and apply them to your own life as I sing them to you.

Elaine Littau

"Alas and did my Savior bleed, And did my
Sov'reign die,
Would He devote that sacred head for such a
worm as I?
At the cross, at the cross, where I first saw the light,
And the burden of my heart rolled away
It was there by faith I received my sight,
And now I am happy all the day."

Mary listened intently. She hadn't personalized the stories
from the Bible to herself. She was a "worm"!

"Was it for crimes that I have done, He groaned
upon the tree? Amazing pity, grace unknown,
and love beyond degree!"

Yes, I am guilty of crimes to those children in my charge! Tears
threatened. *Could Jesus have pity and love for me? How can I
earn this forgiveness?* Her mind was churning. There would be
no way of making up for the things that she had done.

"But drops of grief can ne'er repay the debt of
love I owe."

The melody slipped away as Reverend Hall finished the
song. Mary managed to keep her composure. She decided that
she was going to be thinking about the words of that song for
a spell. She needed to know if they applied to her.

Fred Young took determined steps up to the pulpit. He
held out his hand to his friend for a hearty handshake. He felt
as if he were a drowning man given a lifeline. He lingered with
the handshake as Marcus said, "This man of God is Reverend
Fred Young. You will learn to know him as a man with a message straight from God to you. Listen to the words he says with

your heart and your mind. There is plenty of food in them for both." With that introduction to the church folk, he left Fred and sat with the congregation.

Fred smiled and bowed his head in a prayer to his Father, his Friend. "Dear Lord, let me speak only the words You intend and let them hit their mark." He opened his eyes and expected that he would analyze the crowd, but he felt urgent to speak. "Open your Bibles to Luke 4:18.

> The Spirit of the Lord is upon me, because he hath anointed me to preach the gospel to the poor; he hath sent me to heal the broken-hearted, to preach deliverance to the captives, and recovering of sight to the blind, to set at liberty them that are bruised, to preach the acceptable year of the Lord. And He closed the book, and He gave it again to the minister, and sat down. And the eyes of all them that were in the synagogue were fastened on Him. And began to say unto them, "This day is this Scripture fulfilled in your ears."

"I want you to know that Jesus came to this earth to save us from our sin, but also to help us live our lives every day in a way that would bring glory to God. For some folks this appears to be easier than others, but let me tell you that there is not one person who does not struggle. Has there been one person who has lived who has not had sorrow or a broken heart? I believe that there has not been one person who has not caused sorrow or brokenness in someone else too."

Mary suppressed a gasp.

"Look at what Jesus says here: The gospel is for the poor and the rich. He leaves no one out. He wants to heal the brokenhearted. That means that He can take the pain away. You can live without regret and hatred. He came to preach deliverance to the captives. You may be thinking, 'That's not for me. I'm not in jail.' But I am saying to you that many people live in a prison of their own making. They live in the prison of regret, hatred, and unforgiveness. Many things become prisons to us. He came to recover sight to the blind. I know that Jesus healed blind people and He still does, but there is also a blindness in the soul that Jesus can restore sight to. Are you blind to the love God had for us and that while we were yet sinners, Christ died for us? We become blind to the needs of others. We become blind even to our need for a Savior. There has never been a person good enough to come to God without Jesus. Never. Like the song Reverend Hall sang says, 'drops of grief can never repay the debt of love I owe. Dear Lord, I give myself away 'tis all that I can do.' Give yourself to Jesus. That is all that you can do. There is no way to make up for the unrighteous things, the sins, in your life. The only way to have peace and salvation is through giving yourself away to Jesus. He will set at liberty them that are bruised. To be bruised is like being completely crushed and shattered in life, broken. Do you feel broken? You can be set free."

Tears ran down Mary's chin. She was tired to pretending to be someone else. This man seemed to look at the ugliness in her very being and not be alarmed at it. There was a remedy to the way she felt. What was she supposed to do now? She didn't know how to "come to Jesus."

Fred urged the group, "If you want Jesus, come to the altar now. Do not wait. Come now."

Before she could think of what the women of the church would say, Mary came to the front with baby Sammy in her arms. Reverend Hall's wife put her arm around her and said, "Let me hold the little one for you, Dear."

Mary knelt at the altar and cried like she had never allowed herself to cry before. A number of others joined her in needs of their own. Brother Marcus knelt beside her and spoke softly in her ear, "Talk to Jesus as a dear friend. Tell Him all of your sins. If you don't remember them all, He does. Then ask Him to cleanse you and forgive you of all of them. They will be taken away. I will be back in a bit so that you can do this. I must pray with Widow Grace now."

Mary confessed terrible things that she had done in her life. She confessed every hateful thought and deed. She confessed every disappointment and hurt—things that were monumental and things that were trivial. She asked Jesus to remind her of everything that she might have done that was not right and good. She even confessed for pretending to be different than she was. When she came to the end of all the things she could think of, Brother Marcus was next to her. "Mary, you have repented of your sin. You have done a good thing here, but now you must believe that you are forgiven of all those sins."

Mary lifted tear-streaked eyes to her pastor. "How can He forgive me? I can't forgive myself."

Marcus gently spoke, "Mary, the Bible says, 'For all have sinned and come short of the glory of God.' There is not anyone that deserves to be forgiven. He forgives us because He loves us."

"How?"

"Mary, do you love that baby boy of yours?"

"Yes, of course I do."

"Did he actually do anything to deserve for you to love him besides be your child?"

"Well, no. I do love him."

"You asked God to forgive you of all your sins. You are now God's child. He loves you and wants you to love Him back."

"He loves me?" Mary thought for a moment, "I am His child and He loves me."

"God has forgiven you. Now you must forgive yourself. Let God show you how."

Fred finished praying with the others who had come forward and dismissed the meeting. Mary hadn't noticed she was at the church alone with the Halls and Reverend Young.

Fred softly said to Mary, "The angels in heaven are rejoicing that you have come home to God!"

Elaine Littau

"Really?"

"Yes, will you let me say a prayer over you and you can continue praying after I finish."

"Yes"

"Father, thank you for this young mother who has come home to You. Give her strength to live for You and serve You with all of her heart. She has offered her life to You and wants to be a true woman of God. Amen."

Mary didn't really know how to pray out loud but this nice preacher wanted her to so she would try. "God, I told You all the bad things I did. I am sorry for them all. I will do better from now on. Amen."

Brother Marcus took Sammy from his wife and handed him to Mary. "Mary, Esther and I would like for you to come by the house after chores every day so that we may help you get on in your life with Christ."

Mary smiled and said, "I will do my best. Sometimes I cannot get away...My husband and chores and stuff."

"Come as often as you can."

"I will." She turned and looked at Fred, "God bless you for coming here!" Mary picked up the flour sack that held the extra diapers and headed for home.

"Marcus!" Fred grabbed his friend and sobbed. "I feel as if I got saved all over again too!"

Esther joined in the hug and they all went to the parsonage to finish their visit.

The stars seemed larger and the air was...how could she describe it? Rare. Yes it was rare, wonderful, the breath of angels. Sammy snuggled down into her arms. Could it be possible that she felt even more love for him than before? She hardly believed that it would be possible. She entered the farmhouse through the kitchen door. It was warm and cozy. The big wood stove was still warm from the supper that she had prepared before the special church meeting. She lay Sammy in the basket beside the large oak table and lit the coal oil lamp. It sent a happy glow around the room. Sammy was quietly sucking his fist in his sleep. She pulled the rocking chair close to the stove and placed a few pieces of the split firewood in through the top. Gently she picked up her baby and wrapped his quilts more closely to his little body as she began to nurse him in the quiet of the room. It seemed to Mary to be a blessed time of quiet. She leaned her head back against the high back of the rocker and contemplated the events of the evening. For a brief moment she thought about the women of the sewing circle and what their opinion of her would be now.

"No, I don't care what they think of me anymore! I wouldn't trade gold for the feeling I have inside me right now!" The sound of her voice startled her somewhat. Did she even sound different? She looked down upon the infant who was contentedly nursing, "You have a new Mama, sweetie. I don't have to pretend anymore. I feel good. I feel clean. I don't feel the all fired anger I had all the time anymore." A chubby little hand reached up to touch her nose and she began to laugh. "You darling little boy! Mama loves you so much!" She began to sing, "At the cross, at the cross where I first saw the light and the burden of my heart rolled away…hmmm…mmmm.… mmm…and now I am happy all the day."

Try as she might, she couldn't remember all the words, but the message was burned into her heart. She rocked in her big old rocker until daybreak, humming and laughing. She began talking to God. She hoped that she was doing it right, but she talked to Him as if He were a friend sitting in the room with her. She told Him how grateful she was for His forgiveness. She thought of Sammy and thanked God for him, even her husband. She asked God to help her tell her husband about what had happened to her. She wondered what he would say. Fear began to creep in, but she refused to let it stay. She had been unhappy too long to give up the peace and joy she had just experienced. She had been through many things in her life and if Mr. Dewey wanted to mistreat her, so be it. He could never take Jesus away from her. Memories of her childhood flooded her mind. The bad ones threatened to steal her joy. "Jesus, help me keep joy! Take care of these bad things that happened in the past." The thoughts slipped away as quickly as they came. She remembered things that she had long forgotten. She remembered riding her old horse to school on a warm day. She remembered the smell of the horse in the sunshine. She decided that she liked the smell. Or was it that she loved that old horse? She remembered sliding off him onto a rock in the middle of the creek and splashing water. She had watched the small little fish that gathered around the rock. She picked up one of the smooth stones from the bottom of the creek and felt it. It was brown and shiny. She skimmed it across the deep, still side of the creek and watched it skip once, twice. A smile played on her lips at the memory. "Thank You, Lord, for reminding me that everything in my life has not been hard and bad. I expect that things will go a sight better now with You around."

The first streaks of dawn broke into the kitchen and Mary placed the sleeping baby into his basket in the kitchen. She stretched unhurriedly and completely. She pumped the water for a pot of coffee and stoked the fire in the stove. She added more wood and measured grounds and placed them in the pot. There were still a couple of eggs in the basket so she decided to cook them before gathering eggs and feeding the chickens. She would milk the cow after breakfast this morning. She ate the satisfying breakfast and finished a second cup of coffee while she nursed Sammy. Afterward she tied him in a sling across the front of her so that she could do chores with both hands. Sammy seemed to enjoy the closeness of his Mama. She milked the cow and led her into the pasture where the rest of the small herd fed. Her favorite chore had been gathering eggs. She took the old basket from the hook and began her work. The old girls were really producing today. She fed and watered them and went to the house. She finished her chores with pains of perfection. When she finished and gave

Sammy a quick bath and changed his clothes, she headed to her pastor's home.

Esther answered the timid knock at the kitchen door. "Mary, how good it is to see you this morning!"

"The Parson asked me to come after chores to get some instruction, Mrs—"

"It's Esther, Dear. Yes, Yes, of course, come sit down. Coffee?"

"Yes, please."

Esther glided across the room and addressed her husband, "Marcus, Mary is here."

Marcus came through the door with a sunny smile on his face. Fred followed him into the room. "Mary, I am so glad you came here today!"

"I want to do things in just the right way, Parson. I have lived wrong for so long I want to do this right."

Marcus, Fred, and Esther joined her at the table.

"How do you feel about the decision you made last night?"

"I feel so good. I couldn't go to sleep all night! I had to just thank God all night long."

"I know how you feel," Fred joined in. "I didn't sleep much last night either. I was so happy for you."

"You were? I thought you would be used to showing people the way to God, being a preacher and all."

"It never gets old. Mary, is it?"

"Sorry, Fred, this is Mary Dewey. Mary, this is Fred Young."

"Dewey. Well it is good to meet you, Mary." Fred's mind was racing. *Could this be the stepmother who mangled Nan as a kid?* He forced his face to remain friendly as he listened to the exchange between the parson and new convert.

"What happens, now Reverend. Hall? What do I have to do now?" Mary looked determined.

"Pray every day. Read your Bible every day."

Elaine Littau

"I don't really know what to say to…uh…God. I don't have a Bible." She thought of Nancy's Bible that she had sent away in the trunk and wished that she still had it.

"Just talk to God about every thought that comes into your mind. If it is a problem, talk to Him. If it is a happiness, tell Him. If you have a need, tell Him. He is right at your side all the time. I have a Bible I can give you that belonged to a friend of mine who passed away some years ago. He would want a new convert to have it. In fact, it has notes written in all the margins. You will find them helpful as you read. They will help with understanding."

"Brother Marcus, I have been so bad, is there anything else I need to do to get rid of all the bad things, sins I have done?"

"Jesus died for all of your sins. He paid the price you owed. You cannot add anything to the sacrifice He made for you. If you could then you wouldn't have needed Him and He wouldn't have had to die on the cross. The blood He shed for you was enough to cleanse you and everyone else who comes to Him from every sin ever committed."

"I know that I have tried to turn over a new leaf and be good, but something always happened to mess my plans up. Will being 'saved' work better than that?'

Esther smiled warmly, "Dear one, now you have Jesus living inside of you to help you live a godly life. You don't have to do it all alone. None of us could live a righteous life with out Jesus."

Mary sipped coffee from the cup thoughtfully and absorbed the information. Fred was amazed at the candor and simplicity of her faith. He wondered what Nan would think if she could see her like this. He knew in his spirit that Mary's conversion was genuine. He only hoped that Nan would soon come to God also.

"I best get on with the day. I hope I didn't take up too much of your time." Mary sprang to her feet. Time had gotten away from her.

"Esther, get Thomas' Bible out of the drawer for Mary, please."

Esther gave the worn book to Mary, "In this book are the answers to life. Spend much time reading it and you will keep the peace you found last night. It would be best to begin with the New Testament."

"Thank you, Esther, Parson, Brother Young."

She could hardly wait to get her baking done so that she could open the prized gift. She half ran with the Bible and Sammy in her arms all the way home. Each were precious gifts from God.

Elaine Littau

Chapter Twenty-Four

Nan hummed as she kneaded the bread that the family would have for supper. She buttered the large yellow bowl, placed the soft lump in it, and draped a large white flour sack towel over it to keep flies off. Martha had instructed her to let it "double" and then "punch it down" once more and divide it into two loaf pans. She mentally calculated the time the whole process would take and when she would need to place the pans in the Home Comfort Range. By her estimations Fred would arrive just as the fresh aromatic bread made its way to the table. This morning Martha had opened some of her home canned apples and rolled out pie dough for fresh apple pie. It was cooling on the windowsill.

Nan guessed that Martha was anxious to see how the special meetings had gone. She contemplated the life of a preacher's wife. From what she had observed at the quaint little church they attended, the office of "pastor's wife" was a hard row to hoe. Sister Gracie Brown tended sick folk, brought food to the recovering, taught a Sunday school class, and basically knew everything about being godly. Nan knew almost nothing about being godly or if she was even interested in that sort of life. *Why couldn't they just be "normal folk"?* She didn't mind going to the little church, but she didn't think she had the stuff it would require to be a pastor's wife. Perhaps Fred would be a traveling evangelist. That might be better. No one would expect all that much from her, except Martha told her that sometimes the meetings lasted weeks on end. She would either have to go with him or live without him for the duration.

Martha told her that Elmer could stay with them to go to school whenever she accompanied Fred to his meetings. It would be difficult to take Teddy at this age. It might work out after he was out of diapers. By then there may be another child.

As she mulled these thoughts over in her mind she came to the conclusion that God was taking her husband away. She would have a part-time husband and Teddy would have a part-time father. She felt anger running through her blood. They had been studying about Moses in Sunday school. They had a lot to say about Moses but what about Mrs. Moses? The teacher said that she was stuck home with her father and sisters until they made their way into the wilderness. How long had she been alone? How many young'uns did she have? Did God not have compassion on her? Fred had told Nan that he was "called of God to minister." What did that make her? Just Nan? Fine, he could have his God and his ministry. She lived without him before. She determined to not let the separations affect her. Martha and Nate loved her. She also had Elmer and Teddy to love and look after. She would always love Fred, but from this point on she wouldn't get lonely for him. It appeared that he had made his choice. He chose God's work for him over her and their family. The more she thought about it, the more hurt she stored up inside. As she worked herself into frenzy other soothing thoughts tried to find their way into her mind. *I love him. He rescued me and has been so patient and tender with me. He helped me find a way to help Elmer. He loves Teddy.* Then the other thoughts countered. *If he loved you so much he couldn't leave you. You aren't good enough for a man of God. Who do you think you are?* Her mind was twisting inside, so much, that she developed a headache. She had stewed around so long that it was time to get the bread into the oven. She washed her face in cool water and willed herself to be pleasant because this supper meant so much for her beloved Martha and Nate.

Teddy woke and she retrieved him from his cradle and brought him into the kitchen to nurse and keep watch on the bread and the street. She held the little boy close to her face and inhaled the scent of his hair. He snuggled close and began nursing. Teddy was filling out nicely. He had discovered his hands and practiced reaching out to his mother. He managed to snag a ruffle on her blouse, which seemed to amuse his little

Elaine Littau

mind. He stopped sucking and locked eyes with his ma and gave her a big grin. Milk dribbled down his chin. "How can I get myself into a tizzy as long as I have you? Look at you! You will be grown before long! Mama loves her little Ted." The smile of her son brought a measure of comfort to the turmoil inside her. Her head quit throbbing.

Shasta announced the coming of the traveler and Nan heard Fred's boots crunch the gravel as he walked up the path to his childhood home. The smell of hot bread wafted up to greet him on the little pathway and he decided to make his entry by way of the kitchen.

Elmer was the first of the little company to reach him. "Hey Fred, wanna go fishin' tomorrow?"

"Elmer, let Fred catch his breath! Son, how was the meeting?" Nate took the carpetbag and surveyed the demeanor of his son.

"Great Pa! It felt right to be in the pulpit again."

Martha threw her arms around his neck and gave him a tender kiss on the cheek. "My dear boy. I am so happy for you."

"Thanks, Ma."

Nan remained seated in the chair tending to Teddy. She smiled shyly and said, "It is good to have you back again. How was Campo?"

The words were delivered nicely but Fred paused as he contemplated the meaning behind them. He took two long strides and landed on his knees at her feet. He kissed the pudgy cheek of the sleeping baby. "Sweetheart, I couldn't wait to be home with you!" He enveloped both of them in a warm embrace and kissed her softly on the lips.

"Come children, our supper is done. All we lack is setting the table," said Martha.

"Here, I can get that done double quick!" Elmer offered.

"Let me assist you Elmer, ole Pal, ole Pard, ole friend of mine," laughed Fred.

Nan took Teddy to the bedroom, placed him in his cradle, and joined the family at the large round table. "Preacher boy, you say the blessing tonight."

"Sure thing, Pa."

"Father, thank you for your presence with each one of us at all times. I am truly thankful that whether I am coming or going, You are with me. I am also thankful that at the same time You can be with the ones I love most in my life even when I am absent. Bless the wonderful food spread before us. I thank You for the dear ones I was born to and the precious family that I found. Let us live our lives acceptable to You. In Jesus' Name, amen."

Tears gathered in the corners of Nan's eyes. She couldn't believe how much Fred's words affected her. She was glad to see him. She leaned to him and he thought she was going to whisper something in his ear. Instead he was delighted to feel her soft, sweet lips brush his cheek. Now it was his turn to blink away tears.

In his prayers during the train ride home the Lord impressed him to be careful in his treatment of Nan. He knew he needed to tell her of Mary's conversion, but he shouldn't be in too much of a hurry to just blurt it out to her. She and Elmer had suffered much at the hands of their stepmother and letting go of hurt was a sight harder than getting over anger. He also sensed that Nan was unsure of having a preacher for a husband. She was still trying to get used to having a husband. She was a shy wife, but very loving. He smiled as he remembered the way she snuggled his back when he slept on his side. What a pleasure it was to enjoy her tender embraces. He stole a lingering look at her seated next to him at the table. Her shining dark hair was tied loosely with a pink ribbon. She looked over at him while she buttered a slice of the warm bread. He was blushing! She blushed also as she handed him the bread and said, "Welcome home, darling."

He held her in the circle of his arm, as they lay in their soft featherbed. She placed her ear over his heart and listened to the strong steady rhythm. She felt safe and loved. She hoped it would be a while before he went for another meeting or for a full-fledged revival. *I haven't even heard him preach before.* She mused. "Are you a good preacher?"

"The best!" he laughed

"Seriously, do people really listen when you preach?"

"I don't know."

"How could you not know?"

"I don't pay a lot of mind to the people in the congregation. It works better for me if I just focus on God and what I think He has in mind for me to say."

"I see."

"You will have to hear me preach sometime, dear wife."

"I will. I promise I will."

"Nan, I have been praying about this a lot. We need a lot of time together at this time of our life."

Nan could hardly believe her ears.

"I don't want to leave you for weeks at a time. I want to enjoy you and raise our son and brother. I want to help my Ma and Pa."

"What about your calling?"

"I still have my calling. I will just be careful that the meetings I hold are the ones God has planned. In the summer time I might go for a few days, but I want you and the boys to go with me. I am fortunate that you all are such good campers."

"Campers?" Nan asked.

"Yes, we can take the horses and sleep outside in the warm weather. We would be gone a few days at a time. We could be at our camp in the day and have meetings in the evening and sleep under the stars."

"What about diapers? How would all that work?"

"The Indians wash clothes in the streams and use branches to dry things. I imagine that would work."

"Maybe for a couple of days..." It sounded like a lot of work but it also sounded enjoyable.

"If we go far away, we could take the train. Ma and Pa will watch Elmer and you and Teddy could join me. Most of the pastors have large homes with a bedroom designated for visiting evangelists." He didn't mention that children normally slept in the barn or porch in order to clear a space for him.

"Stay with strangers?" Nan was unsure.

"We are all God's family. It will be alright," He suppressed a yawn.

Nan was a little nervous about the thought of staying with people she did not know, but it might be interesting to see faraway places. She was going to say something more, but was interrupted by a soft snore. She grinned and pulled away from him easily while pushing on his left shoulder. He obediently turned to his side and the snoring stopped. She pressed herself against his back and rested her arm on his side, letting her hand dangle on his chest. In his sleep he found the hand and held it. He was dreaming sweet dreams of the woman he loved.

Chapter Twenty-Five

Nan wiped her hands with the damp dishtowel as she retrieved the dishpan from the dry sink. She used the dishwater to give moisture to the rose cutting Martha gave her. It was planted next to the back step and watering it was the last of the morning rituals in the neat little kitchen. She hummed as she hung the dishpan on the nail next to the back door. She heard a timid knock on the front door. Nan untied the ample white apron and placed it across the back of the closest chair. She smoothed her hair and the front of her dress and buttoned the little buttons around her wrists as she made her way to answer the door.

The second knock was delivered a little more boldly. Nan eased the door open and realized one of her worst nightmares had come to pass. She suppressed a scream before she crumpled to the floor. Mary Dewey stood in stunned amazement on the front porch of Reverend Fred Young. Quickly she knelt down at the young woman's side and looking up, cried for help.

"Nan, is that you?" Fred covered the walkway to the front door in three steps. He picked Nan up and carried her to the rocker beside the front window. "Darling, wake up. I'm here!"

"Fred?"

"Yes, dear."

She began to open her eyes. "She came here! She is here! Oh God, what am I going to do?" Nan covered her face with her hands and began to cry.

Mary stood quietly just inside the door. "Reverend, I didn't know! I came to talk with you."

Nan looked from Fred to Mary. "Why would she want to talk with you?"

Mary cleared her throat "Nan, I came here to talk to Brother Young about my past. I was afraid to tell my preacher about how rotten I was. I know God forgave me, but I didn't know if he should know all the...you know, bad things I done." She continued, "I been thinkin' about you and Elmer, too. I know I am the last person you would ever want to lay eyes on after the bad treatment I handed to you. I want you to know that I am ashamed of myself." Mary began to cry as she tried to hush the wail of baby Sammy, who until he cried had gone unnoticed.

Nan sat in unbelief as she blinked back tears. "What are you up to, Mrs. Dewey? And how do you know my husband?"

"Brother Young is your husband?"

Nan nodded.

"I came forward at the meetin' Brother Young held at Campo a couple of months ago. I made my peace with God. My pastor and him prayed with me and showed me how to get saved."

"You saw her?"

"Yes, at first I didn't know that she was your stepmother. When I found out her name I...well...I didn't know how to tell you that I saw her."

Mary's eyes widened, "When did you find out who I was?"

"The morning Brother Hall introduced us."

"Why didn't you say something?" Mary bounced Sammy on her hip to comfort him.

"I didn't know what to think. I did see that your conversion was genuine. I thought you had enough to think about that day."

"Why didn't you tell me?!" Nan stormed.

"You don't know how many times I started to tell you but I lost my nerve. We have been busy moving into our house. I just hated to upset you."

Nan rubbed her throbbing head.

"Nan, may I come in and talk with you for a little while?"

"I don't know..."

Elaine Littau

"Come in, Mary." Fred stepped aside and offered a straight-backed chair next to Nan.

"Fred?"

"Nan, you must meet this head on if you ever want to get past it."

Mary sat on the edge of the chair with Sammy on her knees. "Nan, ever since little Sammy was born I have been thinking on you and Elmer. When I look in his little innocent eyes I think about how much I love him and how bad it would be if he ever had a stepmother like I was to you children. I was willing to let sleeping dogs lie, that is, until I found Jesus. Every time I pray I see your little back all bruised and bleedin' and I know I was the one who done it."

Nan watched her tormenter carefully to see any indication of insincerity.

"I wanted to talk to your husband to see what I should do to make up for...the cruelty. I honestly didn't know you lived here! I promise! I just need to tell you I am sorry. I know you can't or won't forgive me. I don't blame you if you don't. I don't deserve anything from you. I am just so glad that God forgave me! I want you to know that I am a better woman now. I will never do anything to hurt you again."

"What about Mr. Dewey?"

"I won't tell him where you are. He hasn't taken kindly to your escape and I haven't told him about me finding God. He knows something is up, but he don't know what yet. I have to tell you that to keep him from looking for you I said that I sent you to an aunt in Boston that told us we could have the farm. I know now that I stole it from you by saying that, but in my heart I wanted you to get to safety...away from me and him too."

"You weren't looking for us?"

"No. I don't understand why I kept beating you." Mary began to sob. "I was so miserable I guess I had to inflict misery on you kids. I am worthless for what I did to you. I am very sorry. Fred, what can I do to get away from my past?"

"You have done a great thing to admit to your wrong actions and apologize for them. That is the first step. You have no control over Nan's ability to forgive you. You must continue to read your Bible and spend a lot of time in prayer. Go to church and confide in your pastor. I know Marcus Hall and he and Esther will love you no matter what happened in your past. You will need them to help you when you tell your husband about your conversion. I think that you need to leave now and give Nan some breathing room. I will walk you to the hotel or train station."

"We will be going home on the evening train. I am to meet up with Mr. Dewey to do some business in town. He thinks I have been shopping so I best go before he finds to the contrary."

"I will walk with Mary to the general store and be back shortly. Nan rest in the rocker while I am gone and we will talk this out when I get back."

Nan stared blankly as the man that she loved walked out her front door with Mary Dewey.

Chapter Twenty-Six

Mary walked in silence as Fred escorted her to the general store. She was stunned that while searching for Brother Young she had found Nan and that Nan was Brother Young's wife. It was a lot to take in.

"Are you all right, Mary?"

"I guess...I...Will she be all right?"

"God is watching over her. She will be fine...eventually. You do know that you will have to tell Mr. Dewey about your conversion."

"I know. I have been putting it off. He has a vile temper and I don't want to rile him."

"Ask God for the words to say. He will help you."

"Here we are, Brother Young. Thank you for the advice." She gave a small nod and crossed the floor of the store to the bolts of fabric. It wouldn't do for Mr. Dewey to see her talking with another man.

Mr. Dewey spied her as she edged her way to the button boxes. She seemed to be in deep thought choosing tiny mother of pearl buttons for a baby dress for Sammy. He thought, *"Good, she looks like a doting mother."*

His mother's lawyer set an appointment to inspect the child and Mary in a couple of hours. 'Mary, lets go to the restaurant at the hotel and get dinner before we go to see Mr. Fields."

Mary looked up from the buttons and nodded her head. "Yes, Mr. Dewey." She held the sleeping baby closely and followed him out to the street and on to the restaurant.

"I know it is a splurge to eat in here, but we must look our best when we meet with that confounded lawyer."

The waitress took their order and they sat waiting for the food to come. "Was Mr. Fields agreeable to you, Sam?"

"He is a tightly wound little man. He wants proof that I am married and that I have an heir. I am glad I brought the marriage certificate." He produced the paper from the inside pocket of his suit coat. "I also have a letter from doc stating that he delivered Sammy. That should be enough for anyone."

"Why does he want to see Sammy and I?"

"Because the will says that he must see my wife and boy child before the inheritance is mine. He has to talk with you and ask you about my son."

"You mother wrote all of that in her will?"

"She was thinking of the best for me." He shifted uncomfortably in his chair and started to make a biting comment when the waitress placed a plate of steaming hot soup before him.

"Of course she was. I can understand now how a mother loves her child and wants the best for him."

Sam spooned the soup into his mouth and studied his wife as she shifted Sammy in her arms so that she could eat. She was very tender with his son. It was amazing to observe a woman who had the most vile, caustic tongue tending the toddler this way. He had to admit that of late she had been mild with him too. It didn't appear to be the sarcastic cat and mouse game that they had engaged in for the past year. She seemed genuine in her kindness. *Shoot, she even acted happier, even happier than she was at Sammy's birth.*

Last week he had to make sure that it was Mary doing the wash. He heard her singing at the washboard. He usually kept clear when her saw her hauling the heated water buckets to the wash tub because she would carry on in a cursing fit.

Whatever brought about the change in her moods was too good to be true. He reasoned that it could end as quickly as it began. Her sassiness had landed her a good many blows from his fists in the past, but he hadn't needed to get her back in line in quite some time. He had to be sure that she knew that it wasn't because he had gone soft or anything of that sort. He knew that he spoke more harshly than was necessary lately, but she had to be reminded that he was in charge.

The waitress brought them a plate of roasted meat and potatoes. He began with gusto. "Mary, we need to be sure to only answer the questions that Mr. Fields puts to you. Don't go off tellin' him more that he needs to know."

"What do you mean?"

"He don't need to know about Nancy's kids that we took care of unless he asks specifically about them."

The meat stuck in Mary's throat, "What would he ask about them?"

"Well, where they are and why aren't we tendin' to them."

"I see."

"Tell me how you would answer that question. Remember, he don't need to know that we were glad to get rid of them."

"Well, they live with relatives who love them and want to be close to them. Their Ma wanted them to know her family..." Mary was sure that both of those statements were true. She just wasn't sure that stringing them together like that wasn't a lie.

"Be sure that Mr. Fields thinks that we wanted them and all of that hogwash. Otherwise, he will know that we didn't care what happened to them."

"Of course." Mary breathed a prayer, *"Help me, God!"*

Mr. Fields peered over the bifocals perched on his long skinny nose. "So, you packed them off to relatives? Don't you care for those little orphans that were left in your care?"

"I only want what is best for those children, sir! I have grown to love them with all my heart. I feel sorry that they lost their dear ma and pa. I remember reading a letter that Nancy received from her closest aunt that stated that she wanted to know Nancy's children. I sent their things in a trunk and bought tickets to Boston. Those children should be living with people who are kin to them. It was the right thing to do."

"And this child, Clarence Samuel Dewey III, is your own child borne out of your body?"

"Yes sir!"

"Here is proof of the child's birth...a letter from the doctor." Sam produced the valuable letter.

"Everything looks in order here. I need you to sign these papers attached to the late Mrs. Dewey's will. They state that you will never abandon Sam or the child by way of divorce or any other means. You will see to his education. College is required. You will see that he attends church and religious training every week. You will see that every cultural opportunity available in the state of Colorado will be sought out and that he will become a well-bred gentleman. You will do everything in your power to bring out kindness in his demeanor."

"Yes, where do I sign?"

"There, madam. We are finished with your portion of the agreement. However, your signature is required to be affixed to the papers your husband must sign and vow to keep."

"Vow?"

"Yes, Samuel. You are to listen as I read the attached document, swear to uphold the requirements laid out by your mother, and affix your signature to it."

Sam frowned, but he knew that in order to inherit the sizeable fortune, he must comply. He sat quietly as Mr. Fields began to read.

By now I will have been gone from this world
for a good long time. I know that you, my son,
are not going to be happy with the conditions
of receiving your inheritance. I know the fabric
you are cut from. In some ways you are made of
sturdy stuff. In many ways you are weak. Like
your father, you have been somewhat of a bully.
Unlike your father, I was not successful in getting that out of you.

I know that you thought that all the time you
spent doting on me while I was ill, showed me
that you actually loved me and not the money
in my bank account. I may have been sick, but I
was not a fool.

Sam stood so quickly that he knocked over the heavy
leather chair.

"Sit down, Sam. It is required that you hear this!" Mr. Fields
voice boomed.

Sam righted the chair and eased himself into it avoiding the stunned look in Mary's eyes. Sammy stirred and
whimpered, but Mary was able to rock him gently and he
quieted down.

You were required to get a wife and a boy child
to meet the stipulations of this document. I
knew that if it were not required, you would
take the fortune and live your life and die without an heir. You always were a selfish boy.

I can only imagine the torment you put a wife
to. That is why she will have control of ninety
percent of the fortune. You will get an allowance each week. Mr. Fields will deliver it to
you each Sunday noon after you have attended
church. On weeks that you do not attend, you
will miss your allowance. I want you to be
active in raising your son.
A tithe of ten percent of the income of the estate
will be paid each month to the church you
attend. An offering of five percent of the income
of the estate will be given each month to the
smallest church in the town you live in.

"She was insane!! Stop reading this now!"

"Be seated, sir. I have instructions to cut you out completely if you do not do as required by the will."

Sam slammed his body into the chair.

I know that you have little respect for anyone or anything except money. Do you see what money got me? I could have had all the money in the world, but I am still dead. I want you to learn that lesson before it is too late. I have loved you since the day you were born. As you grew I could not believe how you turned out. I am determined that the cruelty inherited by you from your father stops here. Your son will be a fine man one day. As you know, I wanted to meet your wife, Nancy, before she died. I also asked you to let me meet Mary. I would have liked to meet the woman into whose hands I place my fortune. I have asked friends of mine from Campo and they said that she is a strong, determined woman. For the sake of my grandson and the other grandchildren that follow, I hope that she is also a woman of character. Samuel, you must agree to the following stipulations upon receiving your inheritance:

I swear to never drink alcohol.

I swear to never get a divorce or otherwise separate from my wife, Mary Dewey.

If and when Mary Dewey dies, the inheritance belongs to my son, Clarence Samuel Dewey III. It will be held in trust by the law firm Mr. Fields represents until he is thirty years of age.

I swear to support my wife's business decisions

Elaine Littau

concerning the estate.

I will be an example of a gentleman for my son.

I will live a respectable life.

I swear to give up violence in all forms for the rest of my life.

"I never heard of such a thing as this! I don't think it is reasonable or legal to place such baggage in a will! Let a woman rule me! *Never!* Mary Dewey, do you hear me? *Never!* I will not be a simpering fool like my father was! I refuse to bow and scrape for morsels from a woman's hand!"

He grabbed Mr. Fields by the shirt collar and banged his head against the paneled walls. Mary screamed and jumped to her feet to assist the small man. Sam whirled around and caught Mary on the jaw hard with his fist. She lost her balance and landed on the floor. Sammy made a soft landing on top of his mother. They cowered in the corner whimpering as Sam swore and wrecked the small office.

"Sir, you must gain control of yourself!" Mr. Fields pleaded.

"That old woman will not control me from the grave! I tell you I would rather die!" He grabbed a candlestick from the lawyer's desk and covered the short distance ready to deliver a deadly blow to Mary's head when a deafening blast sounded in the tiny room. Sammy screamed as his father crumpled into a bloody mass on top of him. Mary grabbed her little one and tried to soothe him as the life drained from Clarence Samuel Dewey II. The violent died by violence. Mr. Fields trembled as he held the smoking small caliber gun.

Two men burst into the room and quickly surveyed the damage, "Mr. Fields? Put down the gun. George, you better go get the sheriff! And the doctor. Ma'am?"

Chapter Twenty-Seven

"But Nan, listen to me."

"I don't care what you have to say. You chose sides against me!" fumed Nan.

"I am not against you! Don't you know what the pain in your past is doing to you now?"

"I do all right. I just live for today and try not to think about bad times."

"You still scream in your sleep at night. You are still hurting."

"I don't know what it is you want me to do. Am I supposed to become best friends with Mary Dewey? I would rather die!"

"Best friends is not the goal here. If you don't forgive it will continue to eat you alive. Shoot, Nan, I had to forgive her too!"

"It didn't seem to be so hard for you! How could you?" Nan screamed.

"Because God expects me to."

"I can't believe that just because you are a preacher you would have to do that!"

"It isn't because I am a preacher! God expects it of all of His children."

"A good God would never expect that. I don't believe you." She spat out the words.

"It is for our own good. He knows that unforgiveness will eat at you until you are you lose yourself. You become a bitter person. Nan, you are a sweet, gentle woman, but if you don't forgive and move past this pain you will become a cynical person. The sin of unforgiveness will take over your life and you will never become the woman God intended you to be. We have talked about this. Please listen to me."

Elaine Littau

Nan sobbed as her hands covered her face. "The hate and pain are all I have to hang onto now that you chose her side," she moaned.

"No, Nan. You still have me. Hang on to Jesus. Call out to Him and He will pull you through the pain."

Nan reached out to Fred who was kneeling at her side. She held on tight. "Fred! I can't!"

"In yourself you can't, but tell God all about it. Tell Him exactly how you feel."

"I can't do that! God chose her side too!" she cried.

"God is big enough to love both of you. He doesn't choose sides!" Fred spoke firmly.

"Fred! There has been a killing at the lawyer's office! A woman is there asking for you."

"For me?"

"She has a little baby and is crying something fierce!"

"I'll be right there." He turned to Nan, "I think it is Mary Dewey. She and her husband had business in town today."

Martha ran up to the little house, "Nan, it's your step ma. I came to watch the baby so you could go with Fred. She is in a bad way."

"Is she hurt?"

"No, her husband was killed. She can't stop screaming. The baby...it's just a mess."

Nan and Fred ran to the lawyer's office and arrived as the mortician was removing the body of Sam Dewey. Nan shuddered as she saw the familiar face just prior to it being covered up. Even in death the scowl was embedded on his brow. Mary's screams were deafening. She was rocking her crying baby.

"He is bloody, all bloody! He is bloody, all bloody! Oh God, my baby!"

Fred knelt on the floor next to Mary. The child was trying to wrench out of his Mother's grasp. He was covered in blood. "Mary, settle down. Little feller, are you hurt? Mary, let me see him. Reluctantly, she surrendered her beloved son over to the preacher man. Fred began wiping the blood off of his face with his red bandana. There were no wounds on his head. Then he removed the blood soaked clothing from his body. There was not a scratch. "Mary, you baby isn't hurt! Look at him!"

"He's not hurt? Thank you God! Thank you God! Sam landed on him after he was shot."

"Mary, you do know that Sam is dead don't you?"

"He's dead." It was a quiet statement. She was still trying to believe the events of this long day. She looked up slowly into Fred's eyes. "He wasn't ready to meet God. I never told him anything about God. I was afraid." She held Sammy's bare little body closely and began to rock him. She dragged her eyes away from Fred and looked up at Nan and sobbed. "Oh, Nan! I am so glad you and Elmer got away from us!"

Nan looked carefully at Mary. It was odd to look at her with no fear. It was as if she were looking at a pitiful stranger. Her eye was black and swollen and her lip was cracked and bleeding. She had a fair amount of blood on the front of her dress. Some of it was hers, but most of it was from Sam. Seeing her as she sat rocking her naked baby, Nan felt pity for her.

"That was a long time ago." What else could she say?

"Nan, I beg you to forgive me! Forgive me for everything! I am so sorry!"

Tears filled Nan's eyes as she looked at the poor creature, "I don't know how to!" She turned and walked away.

Fred's eyes locked with Mary's. "She is a good girl. She will learn to forgive the past."

"I think I am being punished for how I treated them kids."

"No, remember Mary, you have been forgiven by God. All is well with your soul."

"What do I do now? The body…I guess a funeral? How do I start?"

"Let's get you and Sammy a room at the hotel. Get cleaned up and I will come help you make arrangements."

"Thank you."

Chapter Twenty-Eight

Fred entered the small home and a meal of roasted chicken and potatoes was waiting for him. Martha made Nan eat and take a nap after she returned from seeing Mary.

"Ma, your bread is always the best!"

Martha smiled. "Nan needs tending to, Dear."

"I don't know what to say to her."

"God will help you."

Fred stretched and slowly opened the door to the small bedroom. "Sweetheart, are you awake?"

"Yes, just thinking."

"What are you thinking about?"

"I just couldn't get over how powerless she looked."

"From the things you told me and how she looked, Mr. Dewey was a brute."

"Yes, he was. Back then she was too. Somehow she looked different today."

"You were looking at her from a position of equality today. She doesn't have any control over you or Elmer any longer."

"I know, but her eyes were different today...even from when she was here earlier today."

"I saw it too. She realizes that she is alone again, except now she has a child to raise. I think she has a clear understanding of how alone you and Elmer were when your parents died."

"She really was sorry...for everything, wasn't she?" Nan bit her lip.

"I would say so."

"I don't know how to forgive her," Nan said quietly.

"God knows that you cannot forgive her in your own strength. That is why He will help you. God knows every-thing you are thinking about. He knows all the pain that you have been through, but He wants you to tell it to Him. It is good for you to tell Him. Healing comes from confession. Confessing hurts and pains committed against you and things you have felt about her and Mr. Dewey," Fred instructed.

"God wouldn't accept me if I told Him all the hateful things I have felt about them. I have felt them about God too!" Nan sobbed.

"Tell Him how you felt when your Ma and Pa died. Tell Him how afraid you were. Tell Him everything."

Nan nodded.

"Then, Nan, you have to repent of your sins."

Nan opened her mouth to reply but Fred continued, "The Bible says that no one that has ever lived has been perfect except Jesus. We all have sinned and come short of the glory of God. But if we confess our sins, He is faithful and just to forgive us our sins. Do you understand?"

"Yes."

"After you confess your sins, ask Jesus to take control of your life. When He does, that is what gives you the ability to forgive others."

"I see."

"Then thank Him for saving and redeeming your soul."

"I feel like I need to be alone to do this. Will that be alright or do I need a preacher with me?"

Fred smiled, "Dear wife, everyone stands before God alone. It is a journey that must begin with one soul and one God. I will leave you for now."

Fred waited at the kitchen table like a man waiting for the birth of his first-born child. He heard her crying and struggling…wrestling with God like Jacob of old. Finally, the door opened and a soft-eyed woman stood in a shaft of sunlight coming through the window. She looked angelic. The black hair was glossy and reflected the sunlight. Goodness, she looked like a painting from the big family Bible on the table. A slow smile spread and blossomed across her beautiful face. One big tear tugged at the corner of her eye and was released as her smile widened. "I never felt like this before!"

Elaine Littau